Blood Ties

S.L. Baron

Blood Ties
Print edition ISBN: 978-1-7345598-0-4

Acknowledgements

First, a huge thank you to Tim for putting up with me through this entire process. His support and willingness to let me sequester myself in the office to write and edit and to randomly rant about the writing process is appreciated more than I can express to him.

Thank you to Robert Tomoguchi, K.V. Wilson, and Jimmie Bise, Junior, who support me as patrons on Patreon. I love having them on this creative journey with me!

And thank you to my beta readers. Soleil Daniels, Kristen Wilson, R. Scott Mather, Jimmie Bise, Junior, and Ann Burgess kindly took time out of their own lives and writing projects to read over this book and give criticism.

Also By This Author

Vanilla Blood: A Novella
The Scarlet Destruction
"Effing Dave"
One Million Project Fantasy Anthology

Blood Ties

Part One

"As I speak, terrorist attacks of unprecedented proportions are underway in the Paris area. There are dozens killed, there are many injured. It is a horror...

"In these difficult moments, we must—and I'm thinking of the many victims, their families and the injured—show compassion and solidarity. But we must also show unity and calm.

"Faced with terror, France must be strong...

"Long live the Republic and long live France."

Excerpts from French President Francois Hollande's speech on November 13, 2015

Chapter One

Exit Wounds

"How long has she been like that?" Lucian's hushed question floated into the bedroom as he eased the door closed.

"Bridget called out to me before the news broke in the states. I got here at one and found her. I cleaned some of the blood off, but she won't let him go." Livia, his fledgling and wife, sighed. "She let me into her head."

"Christ…"

Bridget shut out the voices coming from down the hall of her flat while pulling Bastien closer. She remembered the events of the evening well enough without hearing her friend recount it to Lucian, the man she had given immortality over nine hundred years ago.

"It wasn't about religion, Bridget, ma chérie! It was about money."

Bridget adored the passionate way the student discussed history with her. Many a time she asked questions to which she knew answers just to hear the ardor rise in his beautiful bass voice. He knew she knew; he'd confessed he loved the rapt way she sat listening, her emerald eyes on him.

"The King couldn't owe such an amount to the Knights Templar. He arrested them to rid himself." He took a long sip from his Bordeaux. "We're a month late, but we should toast those brave Knights Templar. A Friday the thirteenth so long ago. October 1307." He held his glass high and clinked it against hers.

What a lovely evening, she mused, finishing the wine in her glass. Streetlights softly illuminated the busy street, casting reflections on the windshields of passing cars. The vampire gazed around the rue de Charonne, smiling at the pedestrians passing by the terrace. She glanced at the restaurant's other patrons, listening to their alcohol-animated conversations, before turning back to her lover, the man she would be gifting immortality to that night.

She barely registered the burning sting and the rapid popping sounds breaking the relaxed air as she set her glass down.

"Bridget?"

Then she felt it, hot blood running down her breast. Her fingers groped at the gunshot wound as she fell to the sidewalk. "Bastien? Wha-what?"

He pressed his hand to her shoulder as he knelt beside her. "I've got you, che—" His eyes glazed over in pain and confusion as his lips parted. "Bridg…" His six-foot frame crumpled over her.

Bridget winced as her wound healed. "Bastien?" She turned him over. "Bastien?" Hazel irises stared blankly up at her. "No. No. No!" She shook the body violently, his head lolling side to side. The bullet had gone straight through his heart, killing him. Too late to give him a life-saving drink of her blood.

Chaos erupted at Le Belle Équipe as a feral howl left her mouth.

She inhaled, finding the lingering bergamot fragrance of his Yves Saint Laurent cologne under the stench of death. "They took you, Bastien. They took you from me." She squeezed her eyes closed and sang quietly to the corpse.

ৡ৵৶

"Is that… is that singing?" Lucian whispered, his chest tightening as his sire's voice floated from her bedroom. He recognized the melody though the lyrics had changed to fit Bridget's Pet.

"… bring life to the fire. Cross this river with me, my ebon-haired child…"

Livia covered her face.

He drew Livia to him, comforted by a wisp of her hair tickling his chin. He planted a kiss on the top of her head. "We'll get her through this. I promise."

She tilted her head up, placing a hand over his heart. Doubtful amethyst irises met his. "I'm not so sure."

He held her palm in place as a frigid wave of uncertainty washed through his body. "We have no choice. We have to."

5

৵৽৫

The air in Bridget's flat became charged before Annelie came into view.

"About time." An unmistakable hint of disgust tinged Lucian's mumbled words. He and Bridget's sire had butted heads more than once over the centuries.

Annelie's nostrils flared delicately. She turned quietly, a corner of her wide, rosy lips lifting momentarily. The ring piercing her lower lip *tinked* as her teeth grazed it.

Livia took a stutter step back, the tension between the ancient vampire and her sire causing the fine hairs at the nape of her neck to tingle.

"Lucian." Annelie reached up and gently tucked a stray ash-blond lock of hair behind his ear. Her topaz eyes met his sterling ones. "I was home, in Vegas, and didn't know what happened. Bridget called out to Livia, not me. I wouldn't have known if Livia hadn't told me."

Lucian held her fingers to his face. "Annelie," he whispered, nodding reluctantly. Annelie's raven hair brushed his cheeks as he leaned in to let her kiss his forehead. He embraced her with a relieved exhalation of breath, both thankful for her presence and ashamed of his behavior. The past could be forgotten for Bridget's sake.

The Ancient stood in front of Livia before the younger vampire turned from Lucian. Annelie's fingers slid down her sides, stopping at her leather-covered hips. The tension fled Livia's body as the other vampire's eyes met hers.

Annelie kissed her cheek softly, then blinked like a contented feline though her eyes were troubled. "Please show me."

Livia nodded, her lips parting, as Annelie gently entered her mind. She sighed, thankful she didn't relive Bridget's memories as the other viewed them.

Annelie's strong arms encircled Livia as Livia's knees buckled, her energy slipping away as Annelie slid from her memories. Soft lips touched hers; Lucian's hands cradled her head. "Shh, Livia. I've got you. Drink."

Viscous blood flowed down Livia's throat. She felt herself passed to her sire's hands.

"I need to see *mo cheann beag*, my little one."

Lucian held Livia upright as Annelie disappeared down the hall. He smiled as a soft breath left her lips. "Are you going to make it?" he asked in his lilting Welsh tenor.

Livia's eyes gazed up drunkenly. "She's like a sharp knife through your mind. You barely feel her there, but—oh —you know afterwards." Her tongue flicked a smear of Annelie's blood from her bottom lip. "She tastes of dark chocolate and red wine." Her hand slid to the fly of his jeans. "Remind me what you taste like."

Lucian hummed deep in his throat as he led her towards the guest bedroom, his fingers finding the laces of her corset.

Dim light fell across Bridget's cheek then disappeared as Annelie slipped into her bedroom, gently closing the door behind her.

"I'm here, *Mo Cheann Beag.*" Annelie knelt before her, brushing a lock of Bridget's hair out of her face. She silently studied her and slid into the other's mind.

Bridget knew her sire wanted to comfort her, but she nudged her out nonetheless, not wanting to feel anything as Bastien's body grew rigid in her arms. Empathy and worry reflected in Annelie's eyes, but Bridget looked away.

"It's all right." Annelie stroked her cheek. "Livia showed me what happened." Her voice cracked as her fingers moved to Bastien's face. She closed his eyes and kissed his forehead. "I'm so sorry."

Annelie disappeared from view and slid onto the bed, spooning against Bridget and wrapping an arm around her. *"Kissed by the flames, you are, my love; take my hand and follow. We'll conquer all we see, my love. And bring life to the fire. Cross this river with me, my copper-haired child…"*

Bridget's eyelids grew heavy as Annelie's soft voice thrummed through her body, and she let exhaustion win.

Lucian traced the curve of Livia's ear with the tip of his nose. She mumbled his name as she drifted off, pressing her nude back to his bare chest. He pulled her in closer with a serene sigh. Having her near always melted the tension from his body.

If only I could still have her with me like before. West Virginia is too far from Wales. Maybe... Guilt overcame him. *What am I doing? Ffwrch. Fuck. Questioning this, of all things, when Bridget is... shite, Bridget.*

He inhaled the scents of their lovemaking and her amaretto-kissed-vanilla blood to banish the odor of death from his nostrils. She'd insisted on feeding from one another after tasting Annelie; the love-making that followed helped comfort their troubled minds.

Blood of an Ancient. Perfect aphrodisiac.

Lucian grew hard at the thought of being inside Livia's body. Her hips moved against him in response; a hand reached back, grazing his outer thigh.

The years without her crept in, banishing his arousal. *Damn it.*

Why didn't I help her brother the night I saved her? What a selfish arsehole I was. I had to know what it would do to her. He lightly ran his fingers over the pale scars marring her forearm. *When she found out...* He remembered the look of rage and disgust when she had sent him away.

Losing Livia had sent him on a downward spiral. *I hope I gave poor heroin-addicted Katya release, for all it brought me.* He buried his face in Livia's tangled honey-blond hair as he remembered how his Pet Katya had made him forget his sin against his fledgling. Katya's drug-laced blood had left him weakened, an easy target for the vampire Simon, whose life work was to destroy Lucian. *The month of torture. Burning. Being beaten.* A shudder wracked his body.

Livia's cool hand stroked his leg. "S'right. I'm here," she reassured, her voice languid.

"I'm all right," he whispered, kissing her neck. "Go to sleep." He caressed the curve of her bottom.

She relaxed back into his arms.

He rested his lips on her smooth skin as he closed his eyes.

His thoughts turned to his sire, his heart aching, knowing a loss like she'd experienced wouldn't soon leave her. *Poor Bridget. Eternity only dulls pain so much. We can still feel the sting when we look at a scar.*

Chapter Two

Je Ne Regrette Rien

Bastien slid from Bridget's tired arms.

"Please clean him up, Lucian. She needs to say goodbye." Annelie's voice floated in from the other room.

Annelie returned, lifted Bridget like she was a child, and carried her into the bathroom. Livia, awash in candlelight, sat waiting next to the tub; she pressed her lips to Bridget's temple before helping Annelie peel off her dried-blood-stiffened clothing. They gently slipped her into the steaming water.

Bridget closed her eyes as water sluiced down her hair and back, trying to cleanse her of grief. She let her mind wander as she watched the candlelight play on her eyelids.

❧⋆❦

February 8, 2014

Bridget sat fondling her iPhone as Edith Piaf's voice crooned from the record player.

"It's finished. Don't look. No regrets." She drained the wine from her glass and poured another.

As difficult as it had been, she'd left Sèbastien's apartment an hour before dawn. She grinned sadly, remembering: soft snores escaping his sleeping form; his smooth, young brow with the one jet black curl that appeared without fail when his hair grew too long; stubble beginning to shadow his cheeks; dark hairs curling on his chest. She'd kissed his forehead gently. "Fais de beaux rêves. Sweet dreams, Sébastien. I do love you. Au revoir."

Dearest Bastien, *the message had read,* This cannot continue. Please understand we can't get over our differences, no matter the love we share. Toujours, Bridget. *She hit "Send" then turned the phone off before retiring to her own daily slumber.*

The vampire squeezed her eyes shut, fighting back tears. "Stop it. You know it's the right thing to do. You can't have him."

A hard knock at the door made her drop the phone.

"Coming." Bridget wiped her eyes with the heels of her hands before opening the door. "Fuck," she mumbled, discovering her visitor.

Bastien leaned against her doorframe with one arm up; he tossed his cellphone across the threshold with the other hand. "A text? A fucking text?" Hurt and disgust fought for control of his voice. He ran trembling fingers through his disheveled hair.

"*How did you get my address?*" Bridget clenched her teeth. I've been so careful about him not finding out…

His red-rimmed hazel eyes narrowed, but he ignored her question. "I told you I loved you. You told me the same. Yet… all I deserve is a fucking text?" He tried to push past her, but she stopped him with a hand to the middle of his chest. He studied it. "I forgot how strong you are."

She tried to ignore the thumping of his heart, the beautiful flow of his life, under her palm. "This cannot be. You know why." She gently pushed him back.

Bastien shoved his foot in between the door and the frame before she could close it. "Avec toi, je suis moi." *With you, I am me.*

She peeked around the door, meeting his gaze, before letting him enter. "You know what I am. And now where I live. If you were anyone else, I'd drain you."

"I'd die happy." He shrugged. "I know, Bridget, and my heart is yours all the same." He sat on her sofa with a heavy exhalation, rubbing the dusky stubble on his face. "You've changed my world. Telling me of your life everlasting. Sharing with me the most intimate moments and love. You tease me with these things." His mouth curled into a snarl. "Then you abandon me?" He buried his face in his hands.

Bridget leaned against the closed door, studying the way his back rose with labored breaths as he controlled his sobs. "I…" She steeled herself as he came towards her, placing his hands at her sides, caging her in.

"You told me about Pets. Make me yours."

She closed her eyes, listening to his breathing, the blood flowing through his veins, and the excited rhythm of his heart. Her chin dropped to her chest as she slowly slid to the floor, defeated.

Bastien knelt in front of her and took her cheeks in his warm hands. "Look at me." She heard his teeth grind against one another. "I'd rather you drain every last drop of my life than to live this pain."

Her eyes opened, searching his face. "Tu m'appartiens," she whispered. "You belong to me, Bastien."

Tears escaped down his relieved face. "Merci," he sighed, resting his head in her lap. He cupped her cheek briefly before turning his wrist up.

Breath caught in the vampire's throat as she nuzzled the pale blue veins running under his skin. He inhaled sharply as her fangs penetrated his flesh. The smooth taste of calvados—apple brandy aged in oak—greeted her tongue. She laid his hand on his chest a few seconds later.

Bridget twirled a lock of his hair in her fingers as her head fell back, the warmth of his blood spreading through her.

"Sing to me, s'il te plaît," Bastien requested, cupping her cheek again.

"Kissed by the moon, you are, my love,
"Take my hand and follow. We'll conquer all we see, my love
"And bring life to the fire.
"Cross this river with me, My ebon-haired child…"

Bridget stared at Bastien's pallid face as Annelie and Livia led her into the room. She felt Lucian's eyes on her as she approached the table.

Non, je ne regrette rien, she thought, running her palm over his still chest. *No, I regret nothing, Bastien.* Her fingers played in the short, coarse hairs before gliding up to his relaxed cheek. *How beautiful you were.* She smiled sadly as her eyes settled on his face, remembering their first encounter.

❧

January 4, 2014

Bridget kept her focus on the book in front of her, willing herself not to glance up at the young man approaching. She took a sip of her Châteaneuf-du-Pape as he stopped in front of her small table.

"Bonsoir. Would you mind if I joined you?"

She looked up, studying him. So very French! If only you were carrying a baguette and wearing a beret. Damn, what a proboscis! *His aquiline nose was just that little bit too long for his handsome face.* Mmm. It works for him, I suppose. Tall, dark-haired, but fair-skinned in that native Gallic way.

He set his half-litre glass down.

Bridget lifted an eyebrow. Half-litre? *She met his hazel eyes.* I wonder how my Blood would change that shade. *The color could produce a rainbow when a human was given the Blood: golden amber, lapis lazuli, or the dark green of moldivite.* Stop it! Bad vampire! *"Oui," she answered, closing the book.*

The stranger pulled out a chair and sat down before a flummoxed look spread over his face. "Oui? You... you would mind?" Confusion parted his lips.

She grinned. "Never mind. Now that you're here, company might be nice." She rested her chin in the palm of her hand and waited.

"You're not French, are you?"

"Are you?" she teased, letting her Irish Gaelic accent lace her normally fluent French as she motioned to his half-full glass.

"Of course!" He blew a raspberry. "In Normandy we're known for cidre.*" The young man took a swig then placed the glass in front of her. "Try it."*

The crisp, dry taste of ripe apples greeted her taste buds. "Cidre, of course. Pays d'Auge?"

"Oui. I'm from Lisieux." He took back his glass, finishing the draught. "Apple orchards and cows. To some, it may not be as sexy as vineyards, but it's home." His lips pursed playfully.

Bridget tilted her head side to side. "I do love Pont-l'Évêque." She fluttered her eyelashes.

His dark head inclined. "You are a woman of taste then."

She bit her bottom lip, then held back a giggle realizing the act as her friend's way of flirtation. All those little things you do, Livia, have become mine. It's been too long since those blond locks have tickled my thighs. Me thinks you and Lucian need to pay a visit.

Her attention returned to the stranger. "You've never introduced yourself."

"Have I not?"

She shook her head. "Non."

He laughed. "How very rude of me! Sébastien Descoteaux."

"I'm—"

"Bridget Finn. I know." Hazel irises glided over her.

"Do you now?" She leaned in closer, crossing her arms on the table. "Should I worry?" she asked sotto voce.

A blush crept up his neck. "I've seen you here many times. I finally asked the bartender about you."

The vampire glanced at the bartender, who was busy popping the cork from a bottle of champagne. "Really? I've only talked to him once or twice."

Sébastien's shoulders rose into a Gallic shrug. "He's a nosy fuck. What can I say!"

๛

Bridget leaned in, kissing Bastien's closed eyelids. *I'll never know what color the Blood would have made those.* Her fingers closed around his. *I love you, Sébastien Descoteaux.*

She inhaled deeply, anger replacing her sorrow. She straightened her back, her eyes roaming over the candles Lucian had used to light the room. Every other candle flickered out at her silent command.

From the corner of her eye, she saw Annelie and Lucian turn towards one another and Livia's jaw open.

Bridget relit the candles, the flames dancing before them.

"Holy shit," Livia mumbled, regarding Bridget with fascination and fear. "You're doing that."

Bridget rolled her eyes to the ceiling, holding back tears, as she nodded in agreement.

Annelie wrapped her arms around her, petting Bridget's damp hair. "That's…" She kissed the top of Bridget's head, unable to continue.

"Fury," Lucian softly finished for her as he met Bridget's gaze.

"I want my old job back, Annelie," Bridget stated.

Chapter Three

Past Lives

"What was your old job?" Livia asked before draining the calvados from her glass.

"I… um. Kali called me an enforcer." Bridget avoided Livia's gaze in favor of her own glass. "I destroyed those who threatened our existence, vampire or otherwise."

"You were good at your job, too," Annelie added quietly, humming with pride.

Livia glanced over at Lucian, who shrugged and gave a shake of his head, indicating he hadn't a clue about his sire's past profession. "So for a decade, you and I spent almost every night together, but you never told me?" Livia scrunched up her face. "Well, except the incident with Simon's sire and the, um, time you said you'd…" She cleared her throat, tilting her head slightly in Lucian's direction.

"I think it's not something Bridget likes to dwell on," Annelie said.

Lucian put his hand up. "Wait. You said you'd kill me?"

"You're right, Annelie. I don't like to think about it." Bridget closed her eyes, forcing back the memories of hunting her own kind and the few humans who lacked the good sense to be cautious, and took a few deep breaths before turning to Lucian. "After Livia found out about your indiscretion, I promised to kill you if she did anything to herself. You would have deserved it, love."

Lucian squeezed Livia's thigh. "Right. I... um... hmmm." He avoided the others' faces and mumbled, "Glad it didn't come to that."

"I am, too," Bridget agreed. She sipped the apple brandy, the taste reminding her of Bastien's blood. "It's not about what I said or did in the past anymore. I'm furious... and heartbroken." She gazed over to the sheet-covered form on her dining room table, feeling Bastien's absence deep within her chest. "What's the use of being immortal if I can't protect the ones I love? Innocent people."

Annelie pursed her lips. "The world has always been a horrid place to varying degrees. We've been through more wars than I'd like to count, lost *so* many loved ones." A melancholy breath left her. "What's changed?"

Bridget felt Livia's eyes on her as she collected her thoughts.

"This is different, though. Isn't it?" Livia asked as Bridget met her gaze with a nod. "There isn't a war being fought here. It's thousands of miles away. Bastien wasn't a soldier—he was a student. None of those who died were soldiers. None of them had the opportunity to fight back." A growl left her throat. "Disgusting, wing-nut, goat-fucking cowards."

"Tell us how you really feel," Lucian joked, studying Livia with wide eyes.

Livia's mouth quirked. "Sorry. I've never been big on people who stone women who've been raped."

"My, oh, my. Showing us your bias?" Annelie gave a low throaty laugh.

"Everyone has some. I know it's not all Muslims, unlike so many others. Trust me, I only feel that way about the ones who hurt innocents." Livia gave an amused shrug and turned back toward Bridget. "What do you want to do? What *can* you do?"

"How do you take on an ideology? They blow themselves up thinking they'll meet seventy-two virgins in Heaven or some other complete shite." Lucian leaned back, crossing his muscular arms over his chest. "They're convinced everyone else is an *infidel*." He emphasized the last word with a cartoonish Middle-Eastern accent.

"I listen," Bridget answered softly, a sad smile turning the corners of her mouth up briefly. She swirled the amber liquid in her glass. "It takes planning to carry out mass murder. I just need to let the flood of voices and thoughts come to me and pick out the plans."

"And then what, *Mo Cheann Beag*?" Annelie questioned, concern marking her voice. "There are dozens of bombings and incidents like what happened here every day. You stop them all by yourself?"

Bridget put her glass on the table beside her and squared her shoulders. "No, not by myself. I need your help." She met the eyes of each of them in turn.

The look passing between Livia, Annelie, and Lucian made Bridget steel her resolve and her spine.

"You all think I'm nuts, that it's just my grief." A soft guffaw left her. "Maybe I am, maybe it is. But… why just sit around letting these things happen? We can do *so much*." She squeezed her eyes closed as blood-tinted tears slid down her cheeks.

"What would you have us do?" the other three asked in unison.

Bridget inhaled deeply and opened her eyes to their curious faces. "You'll help me then?"

Lucian raised an eyebrow. "We have to know what you have in mind first."

Livia bit her lip and nodded agreement.

"Then we need Kali's approval." Annelie tilted her head slightly. "Tell us the plans."

Livia pulled the bed sheet to her chest as she spooned against Lucian. "What do you think about Bridget's plan? About us helping?" She turned Bridget's ideas over in her head: stopping bombings, shootings, and stabbings before they could be carried through; capturing the offenders and "disposing" of them; getting to the root of the insanity and pulling it like an invasive weed.

"Ambitious, albeit slightly mad." His chest vibrated against her as he *hmm'ed*. "I've known vampires during every war who targeted certain groups. Annelie had a penchant for Italian Fascists in the Second World War. She never got over her hatred of the Roman Empire." He kissed her ear. "I don't recall any of us going after an entire group to end a war. Though, if anyone was going do it, Bridget would be my bet."

Livia turned over and eyed him. "What do you mean by that? I've seen Bridget motivated before…"

"Motivated is an understatement." His silver eyes darkened. "How much of Simon's sire's demise did she show you?"

"Not much," she answered, shaking her head. "Just the beginning and what made you leave her."

"Lucky, *lucky* you." Lucian smirked.

"I imagine torture is never pleasant." She patted his chest gently.

He avoided her gaze. "No, no it's not."

"I'm sorry. Wrong thing to *ever* bring up." Livia ran her fingers through Lucian's hair, recalling his memories of sunlight searing his skin and Simon's insanity.

He gently caught her wrist and brought her palm to his lips for a kiss. "Let me say this: Anything Simon thought to do to me, Bridget would have made a thousand times worse." His mouth twisted. "She didn't need a month to torture Amanita—"

"Amanita? *That* was her name? That's a genus of mushroom." Livia suppressed a giggle.

Lucian broke down in quiet laughter. "I doubt it was her real name. Probably thought it sounded dark and Bram Stoker-y. Blah, blah."

"Well, some species are poisonous," Livia mentioned, composing herself. "Go on."

"Bridget went after Simon's sire like a hound chases a fox. To me, she seemed to enjoy it. Tormented her relentlessly: sliding into her brain, making her see things, not letting her sleep. Ripped out her throat, broke bones. The fangs, though…" A shiver ran through him. "Never before had I heard howling like it. Bridget tore them out as if they were made of paper. Fangs don't heal, like the rest of our bodies…"

"She didn't stop until she accidentally confessed to knowing Tesni, did she?"

Lucian studied Livia. She knew how much she resembled his long-dead wife.

"No. Bridget ended her quickly then." He laid his head on the pillow, staring at the ceiling. "Did what you did to Simon. Drank her dry and threw her into the coming dawn."

Livia gazed at him, admiring his straight nose and full mouth, as his eyes moved slightly in remembrance. "What do we do now?"

"We have to decide whether or not to help Bridget." He leaned in, planting a kiss on her lips. "At least we can sleep on it."

Chapter Four

The Children of the Night are Calling

Livia turned over to watch Lucian's face as he slept, but her heavy eyelids won the battle a few seconds later.

The sharp odor of disinfectant fought with the metallic scent of blood and the too-human reek of sweat as she stared down at the lifeless body of her brother.

Livia rubbed his cool hand against her cheek. "Evan, you can't…" She let her head fall to his still chest as she wrapped her fingers around his. The air completely left her lungs.

Evan's fingers twitched, then tightly clutched her palm. "Livia?" his voice rasped.

Her clenched teeth rattled as she inhaled deeply through her mouth. "Evan?" she asked, sitting up.

Her brother turned his head as his dark blue eyes slowly opened. A sad smile turned the corners of his gray lips up. "Hey, big sister."

Livia kissed the tip of his nose. "Evan. You're dead."

He hummed. "I know." His hand slid from her grasp to cradle the back of her head. "And you're immortal." His thumb caressed the nape of her neck. "You have decisions to make now. They're coming."

She studied his pallid face. "I... I don't understand. Who's coming?"

He blinked hard as his eyes unfocused.

"No, don't go, Evan." Her hands went to his cheeks. She searched the dark irises. "Who's coming?"

"The children of the night." His hand fell from Livia's head. His face relaxed in her palms as his eyelids slid down.

"Evan?" The breath caught in her throat. "Evan... don't... no... stay..."

Livia's hands flew to her mouth to muffle her labored breaths as she awoke. She inhaled through her nose trying to calm her racing heart. It had been years since she felt the overwhelming emptiness of her brother's death; it now broke over her like a tidal wave.

She carefully slid from the bed, making sure to not wake Lucian, and pulled a sweater over her camisole and panties.

৵৽

Lucian grunted and turned over in his sleep.

The heat and humidity of the upstairs chamber intensified the smell of sick and childbirth.

Lucian tried to stretch the knot from his back with a shiver, despite the room's temperature, then reached for the swaddled baby and pulled the tiny body to his sweat-soaked chest. "Carwyn. You cried only once." His thumb traced the lines of his son's brow. "Your mother—" He choked as his gaze landed on his wife's relaxed face.

"Tesni," he mumbled as his hand reached out to smooth down her tangled blond locks. He placed the small corpse against her as he tried to remember the prayers Father Afan had taught him in his youth. He closed his eyes. "Ave Maria, gratia plena, Dominus tecum. Benedicta tu in mulieribus, et benedictus fructus ventris tui, Iesus. Sancta—" His teeth gritted as he rubbed the back of his neck. "— Maria, Mater Dei —"

"Lucian?" a quiet voice asked.

Not Tesni's voice. She's… gone, he reminded himself, shaking off the question. "Gloria Patri, et Filio, et Spiritui Sancto. Sicut erat in principio, et nunc, et semper, et in saecula saeculorum. A —"

"Lucian," Tesni insisted.

"Not hallucinations," he begged, crossing himself. "In nomine Patris et Filii et Spiritus Sancti. Amen. Please. I can't…" The prayers jumbled into nonsense as they spilled from his lips.

Tesni's cold hand cupped his burning cheek. "Look at me."

He sobbed, his stomach turning to liquid. His eyes opened to meet her big sky blue ones.

"My love, this is no hallucination. I am dead, but you must listen to me."

Lucian's heart broke anew, cold spreading through his fevered body. "No, no, Tesni, no."

Her nails grazed his beard stubble as she turned his head to face her. "Listen to me." The headstrong gaze he knew and adored stilled him. "You must make decisions. For Bridget and for the future. The children of the night are coming. They'll want answers." She inhaled sharply. "Oh," she breathed as she relaxed onto the pillow, her eyes half closed.

"Tesni?" He gripped her shoulders and shook her. "Tesni!"

Lucian snapped awake, tears running down his cheeks. He ground the heels of his hands into his eyes to stop the flow and glanced to his side, but his lover wasn't next to him.

❧

Lucian pulled on a pair of boxer shorts and a t-shirt then stumbled toward the study, shaking his head at Bridget's taste in furnishings. *I'll never understand your love of Rococo furniture, Bridget. So unnecessarily complicated. Give me the clean lines of my Queen Anne any…*

The glimpse of blond hair halted his thoughts as he stepped into the room. *Not Tesni. Christ. Livia does resemble her so.* He inhaled sharply.

Livia glanced up, giving him a distracted half-smile, then returned her gaze to her glass of wine.

Lucian sat beside her, failing in his attempts to push his nightmare from his mind. "Bad dream?"

She took a small sip of wine, then ran her finger around the glass's rim, making it sing softly. "Yeah, um…" She chewed her lower lip nervously.

"Me, too." He laid his head back and closed his eyes. *So vivid… I haven't thought of that day in years. Dammit.* His eyes opened as he turned his head toward Livia. *Looks just like Tesni did: honey hair; that small, upturned nose; lips I can't resist. At least her eyes are different.* She drained her glass as he watched and went to pour herself another. His eyes followed her there and back to the sofa. *By the look on her face, she dreamt of —of course!—Evan.* His stomach cartwheeled. *The worst loss of her life. The biggest mistake of mine.*

The heady fragrance of cloves wafted into the room and turned his thoughts.

"Annelie?" Livia asked softly as the Ancient paused in the doorway.

Annelie met them with a haunted look, then came into the study, set her coffee mug on an end table, and made herself comfortable in an armchair. She took a long drag from her *kretek*, inhaling the smoke.

"All right?" Lucian raised his eyebrows in question. He'd rarely seen her upset in his nine-plus centuries.

"No, no." A shudder ran through her. "I just relived one of the worst nights of my existence in the oddest dream," she whispered hoarsely.

"You, too?" Livia hugged herself.

Lucian ran a hand over his hair. " 'The children of the night are coming…' " The other two vampires stared at him, nodding reluctantly.

"I was told I need to make a decision." Livia took a sip of wine, her hands trembling. "Do the dreams mean Kali's coming?"

"Kali prefers her iPhone to giving people nightmares. She's not one for sending portents of her arrival. Well, not anymore." She snuffed out her cigarette. "I talked to her. She's sending someone here to discuss the situation."

"The children of the night. Here I thought we *are* the children of the night," Lucian mused.

The ancient vampire guffawed. "Apparently we are wrong," she joked darkly, lighting another clove cigarette. "Whoever the children of the night are, if they can invade our dreams, I don't think I want to meet them. The hell if I'm going back to sleep after that horrible memory-nightmare." She tucked her long legs under her and grabbed her steaming mug with her free hand.

Lucian glanced at Livia who gave him a sad grin. "Safety in numbers it is then." She squeezed his thigh gently.

Chapter Five

Secretary

A rapping at the door roused the three vampires from their unintended slumbers.

Annelie sprang to her feet and darted from the room as Lucian and Livia stared bleary-eyed at each other.

"Feeling any better?" Lucian asked, pulling his lover in close.

Livia nestled against him. "I hadn't had a dream about Evan in years. How about you? Tesni?"

"Yeah." His head fell back against the couch. "Bad dreams about Tesni were never an issue. I'm just relieved it wasn't her actual death I dreamt. It took me years to push that to the back of my mind." He glanced down at Livia. "You scared the shite out of me when I walked in here this morning."

She petted his chest playfully. "Like you told me years ago, Mother Nature knew a good thing and recreated it."

He kissed her forehead. "Well, anyway, I wonder who's arrived: The children of the night or Kali's messenger." He helped her to her feet.

❧

They found Annelie glaring at the vampire in the foyer.

"I heard ya were a motley crew but greetin' me in your jim-jammies I never expected." Eyes like chocolate diamonds shifted to Annelie. "Aren' ya gonna introduce me, Annie?"

Annelie grimaced. "I told you to never again call me that, Boyd." Her lip curled. "Lucian, Livia, this is Boyd, Kali's personal assistant." She motioned to the others. "Boyd, Lucian and Livia."

The dark-haired vampire's eyes briefly studied Lucian before alighting on Livia.

What an Aussie twat, Lucian thought, assessing Boyd's khaki trousers, moss green wool jumper, and messenger bag. *Five o'clock shadow? Really? Decided to look rugged for all eternity?* He glanced down at Livia, who smiled warmly at the newcomer. *Well, fuck me. Forgot she can't resist an accent.*

"It's Thaddeus again, *Annelie.* It was time I went back ta it. Thaddeus P. Boyd, at your service. Thad. Or Thaddy, if ya like, Livia. Thaddy. It rhymes with 'daddy.'"

Lucian rolled his eyes. *Twat.*

"What's the 'P' stand for?" Livia asked, seemingly amused by the newcomer's flirtation with her.

"Not a thin'! Both ma parents were transported to Oz as convicts. They thought the letter'd make me sound distinguished." Thad shot her a proud grin.

"Didn't work," Lucian muttered.

Thad studied him with narrowed eyes. "Ya put all that hair inta onea them man buns?"

Lucian straightened to his full six-foot-five height. His head involuntarily tilted down toward Livia.

Thad looked from Lucian to Livia with a wry smile. "Sorry, mate. Didn' realize."

Lucian felt Livia poke his mind. *Jealousy, really?* she questioned silently. He stared down at her, feeling like a puppy who'd just pissed on the floor.

"Could we maybe get back to why Boy—Thad is here?" Annelie huffed.

Thad gave them a lopsided grin. "Too righ'. Where's the little redhead?"

❧

Bridget's insides knotted as Annelie led her into the study. The mixed feelings of the group seeped into her mind as she sat and tried to focus on Thad. She pulled the sleeves of her sweater over her hands and balled up her fingers to comfort them with the soft, warm cotton.

Tears burned her eyes as she remembered how Bastien used to tease her about the habit. *"Ah, chérie, I can warm you so*

34

much better if you let me." His deep, gentle voice flowed through her brain.

She wiped her eyes roughly, then raised them to meet Thad's face. "So?"

"Well," Thad started, leaning his elbows on his khaki-covered thighs and steepling his fingers. "To be honest, Kali thinks ya a bit mad to wanna take on such an endeavor but says gas on."

Annelie wrapped her arms around Bridget and squeezed her tightly. "I knew Kali would approve."

Bridget felt the nervous energy flowing through her sire. "What about you though? And you two?" She tilted her head into Annelie and lifted her chin at Lucian and Livia. "Will you help?"

Thad glanced at the silent group. "Shit, I'm in! Kali sent me 'cause I wanted ta help."

A quiet grunt of disapproval left Annelie's throat as her body stiffened against Bridget.

"Oh, don'cha worry!" Thad waved his hand at the ancient vampire. "I won' be in the way." He leaned back in the chair, stretching out his legs to relax. "I've wondered for years who the hell we'd feed from an' sire if these crazy cockies keep blowing up the best people."

"Great. Just what we need: A secretary taking on terrorists," Lucian groaned.

Livia shot Lucian a perplexed look and met Bridget's questioning gaze. "Of course we'll help."

"Yeah, of course," Annelie chimed in, petting Bridget's hair.

"Where do we start?" Lucian asked, doubt still clouding his words.

Bridget closed her eyes. "I'm going to search for the bastard who planned the attacks here first." Bastien's confused, pained face flashed on the inside of her eyelids; she quickly opened them. "He can hide all he wants from humans, but he can't hide from me." A small smile turned up her lips despite the dull pain she'd been suffering. "Then onto the rest of the world. No one can hide from *us*."

Lucian's mouth quirked as he met Livia's eyes. "With the way you feel about them, I have a feeling you're going to have a little too much fun with this." Livia shook her head in amusement.

Thad clapped his hands and rubbed them together. "I knew I'd like ya all. When do we start?"

Bridget's insides untangled. *I'm going to change this world, Bastien. No one else has to die like you did. Not if I can help it.*

Chapter Six

God Complex

With a rough outline of their strategy completed on the table, the talk turned to lighter subjects, relaxing their exhausted minds, before dawn called them to bed.

Lucian brought his long legs onto the couch and rested his head in Livia's lap as the others discussed the best locales to feed in Paris. He caught Thad's eye, shooting him a quick smile, as Livia ran her fingers through Lucian's hair. He closed his eyes.

❧

Bridget smiled sadly as she glanced down at Lucian. "I think he has the right idea." She rose to her bare feet. "There are busy days ahead." She planted a soft kiss on Lucian's temple and Livia's cheek. "Thad, goodnight and thank you."

Thad acknowledged her with a dip of his head.

"Wait up, *Mo Cheann Beag*," Annelie called, pushing herself up. "I don't think I can sleep alone today. Not after my nightmare yesterday." She wrapped an arm around Bridget's waist as they made their way towards Bridget's bedroom. "Goodnight."

Thad's eyes followed Annelie until she disappeared into the dark hallway. He shook his head as his attention moved to Livia. "Alone at last. Well… almost." An eyebrow lifted at Lucian's sleeping form.

A quiet laugh escaped Livia's lips. "Don't give up, do you?" Thad shook his head. "I've never seen Annelie as flustered as I have this evening. So… you two…" She let the strands of Lucian's hair flow through her fingers absentmindedly.

"That obvious, eh?" Thad's chocolate-diamond eyes watched her fingers longingly. "Years ago, Annie—Annelie —an' I bonded over shared emotions, namely hatred a the shits who sired us." He motioned to Lucian. "He obviously gave ya a choice."

Livia nodded agreement.

"Ya probably knew Annelie didn' choose this life."

"I did." She glanced down at Lucian. "I can't imagine what you or Annelie went through."

Thad shrugged. "My sire was a psycho witha god complex." He laced his fingers together in his lap and stared down at them. "I hadda life… Pregnant wife, little son." His eyes grew distant. "Fuckin', stinkin' Aborigine maniac."

Livia bit her lip uncomfortably, thankful, despite later discovering Lucian's betrayal, her experience had been consensual. "What happened? That is, if you wouldn't mind telling me."

He nodded. "I can' resist a pretty Shelia." He winked as she rolled her eyes. "No, I don' give up, Livia." An amused grunt escaped him. "I madea living as a drover—kinda like what you Americans call cattlemen, I think. People hired us to move herds distances. Not the ideal job witha young family. Sometimes kept me from home fora year, but Ma an' Pa were proud, as was ma wife, Shoni."

Thad sighed, his eyes alight with nostalgia. "We hadda house near Coopers Creek, in Queensland; ma parents lived right nearby. I still see it when I close ma eyes. An' Shoni... her long auburn hair tied back, but one pesky strand always snuck across her cheek..."

The corners of Livia's mouth lifted as she watched Thad reminisce. *The lives we lived before immortality never completely leave us, do they?*

He rubbed his cheek, returning his thoughts to the present. "Sorry."

"It happens." She shrugged and motioned for him to continue.

"The last contract we left on was big. Twelve hundred head a cattle. Seven a us: four stockmen, me included, plus a cook, the boss, and our horsetailer. Standard for the livestock. We usually covered about ten miles a day." He patted his thighs. "Legs like iron."

Livia laughed. "I'm sure!"

"Anyway, we needed to cover a thousand miles. A hundred days didn' seem too awful, I thought, though I wouldn't be there to see Shoni birth our second child. She kissed me when I apologized. 'You only just made it in time for Benji's bottom slap, Thaddy. Your ma'll get me through this one as well,' she reassured me, patting her huge belly." His mouth quirked.

"Everyone always speaks a women, especially back then, bein' such fragile creatures. Dunno, maybe some were. Those I knew—Ma, ma sister, and Shoni—they were tough shits! They had ta be." He motioned to Lucian. "I know he saw it, too. Men died, leaving them lonely. Children died, leaving them all alone. They needed to be strong ta maintain when everyone left them behind."

"It's nice to know you have such a beautiful view of women even though you keep trying to get in my pants."

"Just because I try, doesn' mean I don' respect ya. Besides, ya could easily crush me. I'm far from powerful, like all a ya here.

"Well, ta continue: twelve hundred head cattle, a thousand miles, a hundred days at least. Thirty-one days in an' goin' strong. Only losta handful a cows. Decent water supply. Piece a piss!"

An ironic hum rumbled through Livia's chest. "How sad life seldom remains so."

"Nonea us live carefree forever." Thad stared down at his fingers. "Anyway. The slightest noise can set cattle off in the middlea the night. Chaos reigns then. Ya better make it uppa tree or ya get trampled in your swag. Cows are stupid creatures." His head shook in disgust. "The panic that night didn't seem typical somehow. Sure, men were yellin', screamin', but..." Horror washed over his face. "Then I saw Donal, another stockman. A dark shadow straddled him, its face buried in Donal's neck. As I ran over, the shadow turned to me with rage in its eyes." He shuddered violently. "Those eyes. Black as ink with little bits a color reflected in the lighta the full moon." He ran a hand over his hair, causing it to spike up in odd directions. "I felt the thing ram me, felt sharp teeth pierce ma neck, then I passed out.

"I came to ta sobbin' and more screamin'. There were twenty a us chained together 'round a huge, roaring bonfire." A moue of distaste crossed his face. "The reek a fear... shit an' piss an' ol' sweat. I could taste it..."

Livia's chest tightened. She recalled the night Annelie told her about being sired against her will; the same look of disgust, hatred, and terror met her now. She searched his eyes. "Thad?"

He inhaled with a sharp shake of his head. "Called himself the Aborigine. Insane cunt. He moved clockwise around the chained circle, sirin' each a us in turn, letting the previous writhe in agony as the Blood changed us." Tears glistened in his eyes.

"He sired all twenty of you that night?" Livia asked, her brows knitting together in surprised confusion.

Thad nodded. "I mentioned he had a god complex, didn' I? Huh. He projected his desires inta our heads as he drank from us: a flock of immortal followers. He showed us how to feed an' sire, to kill an' create."

Livia stared down at Lucian. She recalled his weakness following her siring; he'd drained two violent muggers before she had her first meal. "I-I didn't realize mass-siring was possible."

Thad acknowledged her with a lift of his chin. "It's possible. Not recommended but possible." His mouth twisted. "Some a us broke our chains once the Blood ran its course. I found Donal, the cook, Jules, an' our horsetailer, Owen, among the changed. Two or three other fledglings joined us while the others sat uselessly blitherin'. We took control of the Aborigine." His eyes narrowed. "Mass-sirin' makes weak fledglings, but, after giving twenty your blood, it weakens the piss outta ya. Our small group fell on that stinkin' shit like wolves onna deer: drank him dry, ripped his limbs off, and threw the pieces into the bonfire." He ran the knuckle of his index finger down the bridge of his nose and grew quiet.

৵৽৽৻

Livia hesitated before breaking the silence. "What did you all do after? What about Shoni?"

"Hmmm?" Thad's reverie broke. "Oh, Donal, Jules, Owen, and I started back home. What the others did, I dunno. The Aborigine projected what our weaknesses were as he sired us. I doubt all the other fledglings believed what they'd been shown. I'm sure some burnt up as the sun rose." He paused. "It didn' take us long to make it back to Coopers Creek. Newfound speed, I suppose, one benefit of bein' turned into a vampire against one's will.

"We had ta stop ta find cover at dawn, but early the next evenin', I got home." His expression softened. "I watched Shoni through the window. She sat in her rocking chair, our infant daughter at her breast and Benji at her feet playin'. I made for the door, but ma hand stopped halfway there. How the *shit* could I tell them what I was? I hardly knew." Thad laughed. "I waited until Shoni put the kids down for the night and slid inside. I hoped she wouldn't go right for the shotgun, seein' someone there unexpectedly. She stopped short but recognized me and ran inta ma arms. 'Thad, what's happened? You're supposed ta be gone for months. Your skin's freezin'!' She stepped back and took my cheeks in her hands, rubbing my stubble as she liked to do. 'Your eyes…' Thankfully curiosity, not horror, met me."

Livia's eyes widened. "Did you tell her?"

"Yup."

"And?"

"Growin' up in a place with kangaroos and platypuses, ya learn to accept things that seem unlikely. Told ya she was a tough woman!" He chuckled. "It wasn' easy, but we got by. Benji and Lula, our daughter, thought it odd Daddy never aged like Mummy. When they got older we explained it ta them. I became Uncle Thaddy fora few generations. No other way ta stay with ma family." His gaze returned to his lap. "Shoni refused to let me sire her, no matter how I begged. She lived to be ninety-five, though. Suppose that's somethin'."

☞◦☜

"I can't believe you managed to stay with your family! Amazing," Livia breathed.

Thad shot her a mischievous grin. "Ya know what else would be amazin'?"

"Don't even…" She shook her head in amusement.

"Hearin' ya cry out ma name." He glanced down at Lucian. "Then again, both a ya cryin' out 'Thaddy' doesn' sound too awful either."

Livia jumped as Lucian tensed under her hand. He raised an eyebrow at the vampire across from him.

"Knew ya were awake, mate!" Thad flashed Lucian a wide white smile and laughed from deep in his chest.

Chapter Seven

Worlds Collide

The sunset gently pulled Livia from the stupor of vampiric sleep. She always woke earlier when she visited Paris. *The allure of the City of Lights,* she mused. *The museums, the food, Parisian blood flowing sweet with excitement, love, and French flair.*

"No wonder people think we're undead," she mumbled, smiling down at a still-slumbering Lucian. His chest barely rose with respiration, and his face and limbs were coffin-still. She shook her head as she slipped from under the sheets, biting her lip to hold back a giggle. "I can't believe you're jealous of Thad. Men: Even immortal, you remain silly boys."

Livia slid into a pair of jeans and her favorite corset—a plain, steel-boned, black sheepskin overbust one that laced up the sides. At the last minute, she decided to throw on a shrug before heading to the living room. *Maybe some extra coverage will ease that tension growing between Lucian and Thad!*

She found Bridget sitting cross-legged on the balcony's love seat despite the cooling air. Bridget cradled a smartphone to her breast, her eyes lightly closed.

Livia scanned the somber skyline behind her friend, noting how the city seemed gloomy without the Eiffel Tower illuminated. "You're up early," she commented, sliding down beside Bridget.

Bridget met her gaze with a shrug. "So are you." She leaned into Livia, resting her head on the other's shoulder.

"What are you up to?" she asked quietly, putting an arm around the elder vampire.

"I came out to listen for… well, anything, but then this caught my eye." She held up the iPhone. "Lucian put it on top of Bastien's clothes when he, um, c-cleaned him up." The vampire thumbed it on, then slid her finger across the screen to reveal a photo of her and Bastien in front of Notre-Dame. She swiped right: dancing in front of the Moulin Rouge; kissing at the foot of the Eiffel Tower; clinking wine glasses at Le Belle Équipe before the attack. "I told him to delete these. It's obvious what I am. Stubborn frog."

Livia hummed softly, studying how Bastien's face lit up as he looked at Bridget in the photos. "He was a beautiful man." Bridget's head inclined against her in agreement. "Would he have let you sire him?"

Bridget remained silent for a moment. "It was going to happen that night."

A cold, dull ache washed through Livia's chest at the statement. She rested her forehead against Bridget's hair, words failing her.

"He always laughed when I teased him, when I'd say I wanted to find out how the Blood would change those hazel eyes of his. He'd only grin and say, 'One day, chérie, one day.' Then that one day came. He said yes." Bridget paused. "Thank you for deciding to help."

Livia kissed the top of her head. "You got me through so much. How could I not do the same for you?" She moved a copper lock of hair behind Bridget's ear.

"I only pointed you in a direction. This won't be as easy." A heavy sigh left her.

"What you did meant everything to me." Livia inhaled deeply, wondering how the attack's other survivors were faring; the scents of fear, grief, anger, and relief flooded her nostrils in answer. "Besides, I mentioned I dislike these bastards, didn't I?"

Bridget snorted softly. "I believe you referred to them as 'disgusting, wing-nut, goat-fucking cowards.' Do you worry where you are? They hate Americans with a passion, it seems."

Livia's head tilted side to side as she weighed the question. "Things have happened in the States, but I guess we feel fairly safe in Belle Hollow. Half the people are vampires, the other half West Virginians." Her mouth quirked. "Personally, I feel the terrorists should fear the West Virginians more. A nutter goes yelling *Allahu Akbar* where I live, and chances are they'll end up with a forty-five caliber or a nine-millimeter bullet hole. Possibly aught-six. All three depending on the day." Bridget's easy laughter assured Livia her friend was healing. "The natives there take little in the way of bullshit."

Sounds from the kitchen drew their attention as the aromas of brewing coffee and cloves wafted through the doors. "Annelie's caffeine and kretek addiction. Then again, we're both lushes, aren't we?"

Livia's shoulders lifted in agreement. "Easy to have vices when you know they won't kill you." She rose, helping Bridget to her feet. "Come on, let's—" A knock at the door interrupted her. "More company?" she asked as they headed for the foyer.

๛๛

Livia and Bridget found Lucian and Thad already at the door.

"Ahh, c'mon, mate! Sure ya don' wanna cuddle? Or how do ya say it in Welsh? *Cwtsh?* Shit, that's allota consonants. An' they say English is hard ta learn," Thad teased, pulling a sweater over his damp hair.

49

"I swear to Christ, Thad—" Lucian stopped short when he noticed Livia and Bridget. "I'll… just get the door then."

Bridget gave Livia a curious glance as Annelie, coffee mug in hand, joined them. Livia mouthed "later" with an amused grin as Lucian turned the doorknob.

Two young girls silently entered the apartment and closed the door behind them. The mahogany-haired four-year-old wore a dark gold, embroidered *choli* over a wine-colored sari; a tiny, tear-drop pearl *bindi* decorated her smooth forehead. The other, a towheaded girl of seven or eight, wore a navy blue sailor dress, pristine white knee-socks, and her hair in braided pigtails; she carried a messenger bag slung over her shoulder.

The energy radiating from them made Livia, Lucian, and Bridget take small steps back; Annelie inhaled sharply, coffee spilling over the edge of her mug.

"Well, hello, ickles! What're you two doin' out by yourselves?" Thad asked, greeting them with a wide smile.

"Idiot," Annelie uttered, shaking her head in annoyance. The younger girl met her gaze, but Annelie quickly bowed her head, shame darkening her face.

"Hello, Morning Star," the girl said in her Indian-British accent. Eyes like smoky quartz studied each of the vampires in turn.

"Mornin' Star?" Thad glanced from the child to Annelie. "What'm I missin'?"

A heavy breath left the ancient vampire. "Thad, this is Shreya. Kali's niece."

"Holy shit! Shit!" Thad avoided Shreya's face in embarrassment. "Sorry for ma language!"

"Mistress Shreya is nearly five thousand years old," the blonde child stated matter-of-factly, rolling her sapphire eyes. "She's heard a naughty word or two and invented some to be sure."

"Ya mean the *Original Shreya?*" Thad asked Annelie, his eyes wide. *"Shit."*

"Who the fuck else would she mean?" Lucian mumbled, his lip curling to show a fang. "Shreya, the diminutive Bollywood artist?"

Livia furrowed her brow as a volley of insults flew from Lucian to Thad with Annelie's occasional interjection. She noticed Bridget shake her head as small fingers grazed her hand.

"Up, please," Shreya requested of her, fangs peeking out of her soft smile.

Livia nodded as she lifted the girl, resting her weight on a hip.

Shreya observed the argument for a minute, then loudly cleared her throat. "Enough." Lucian, Thad, and Annelie stopped mid-sentence; Bridget turned. "You should have expected us. Did you not have the dreams?"

Shudders simultaneously ran through Livia, Lucian, and Annelie.

The Original's head tilted in curiosity. She pursed her lips and stared into Livia's face. "Were they not happy dreams? Speaking once again to the loved ones you lost?"

Livia met the large eyes, impressed they appeared innocent despite Shreya's age. "To be honest, they were slightly disturbing. We weren't sure what they meant."

Shreya lifted a mahogany eyebrow. "Are you sure they were disturbing? I always enjoy dreams where I see my loved ones again!" Lucian and Annelie's haunted looks answered her question. "Oh, well... Natasza," she said, motioning to the towhead, "make sure to message Ajit and tell him that." She turned back to the adult vampires. "We're here to offer our services in Bridget's crusade. You need us. We need you."

Chapter Eight

Fire Starter

Natasza pulled an iPad from her bag as she headed into Bridget's living room. Shreya, still in Livia's arms, motioned for the rest of the vampires to follow.

Livia set Shreya down in a wingback chair as Lucian, Bridget, Annelie, and Thad took seats on the couches, staring expectantly at the Original. An uncomfortable silence blanketed the room until Annelie clicked her lighter for another cigarette.

"First," Shreya began, sadness in her eyes, "we're sorry for your loss, Bridget. Sébastien was a good man and would have made a worthy immortal companion for you. He loved you well."

Bridget nodded briefly. "Thank you," she answered, slight confusion lacing her voice.

"Second, we're pleased you've decided to take a stand against what's been going on. Together we can finally put a stop to those filthy swine who plague our world. We've come to realize we alone cannot win this war. We need you."

"You and Ajit have been trying to stop these people all by yourselves?" Lucian asked, scanning the inquisitive faces of his fellow adult vampires.

"Not just Ajit and me. All the Children of the Night. We've been doing it for years, in little ways," Shreya answered, her sandaled feet swinging nonchalantly.

"Does Kali know what you've been doing?" Annelie took a drag from her kretek.

"Oh, yes! Though I don't tell Ajit I talk to her. He hasn't gotten over certain actions of our aunt."

"Understood." Annelie winced. "Then why hasn't she tried to help?"

Natasza looked up from her tablet. "Because, vampire or human, all adults are similar. You're oddly indifferent to the world's issues until they land on your doorstep. We, however, being children, cannot help but be affected by them and see how others are."

A palpable wave of shame passed through the room.

Shreya held up her hands. "Don't misunderstand Natasza, please. We see why you're that way. You hide in plain sight very well, with your museums, theatres, clubs, and book signings." She glanced at Bridget, Livia, Annelie, and Lucian in turn as she listed them off. "We find it amazing, actually, how many of you contribute to the culture of this society! It's not the same for us. We can't publicly have those things since we still look like children. We've done what we can, though."

"What's it ya do?" Thad asked, enthralled by the Original. "Kali never mentions ya!"

Shreya smiled at Thad. "Lots actually! Ajit and I started siring other children three millennia or so ago. Children, like we had been, were suffering. Hunger, war, disease, abuse, abandonment. We decided it was our duty to help them the only way we could: turn them into creatures like us."

"You must be legion!" Lucian stated, his brows rising.

A quiet hum left her throat. "Not quite. We don't sire *every* child."

"For some, it's better to end their suffering completely," Natasza announced. She frowned as the adult vampires gazed at her in wide-eyed horror. "It's the same when you sire, isn't it?"

Livia nodded reluctantly. "It is. Hearing it regarding children is… uncomfortable."

Natasza tilted her head in curiosity. "I figured if you knew Morning Star, it wouldn't bother you."

Thad glanced at Annelie then at Natasza. "Waita minute. What's 'Mornin' Star' all about? I never heard her called that before."

"It's what her followers called her." Natasza turned her gaze to Annelie. "In most cases, 'Mourning Star' would have been more appropriate. Though, I suppose you *were* kind enough to only ask sacrifices from families with multiple children."

Disgust darkened Thad's face as he met Annelie's. "Ya fed from kids?" He quickly scanned the others' faces, realizing they already knew, then stood up. "I… um…" He left the apartment without looking back.

Lucian, Livia, and Bridget met each other with uneasy expressions.

Annelie closed her eyes and brought a hand to her forehead. "Damn it."

Shreya hopped from the chair and went to her side. "Let it go." She patted Annelie's thigh gently. "He *will* accept it, forgive you. It may take time. I, after all, came to terms with it and have forgiven you and Aunt Kali your indiscretions." She pulled herself onto the couch beside Annelie, resting a hand on the ancient vampire's back.

"To continue. Though we can't take part in the world like you, we've managed to make a place for ourselves." Shreya smiled proudly. "We've learned to fit in quite well as pickpockets and street urchins in big cities. Here, India, anywhere people are too busy to pay attention or would rather look away from a ragged child." She shrugged. "Otherwise, we do much the same as you. We feed on those who won't be missed. Most of the Children tend to lean toward pedophiles and child abusers, ridding the world of them as much as possible."

"Some of the Children see it as their personal duty," Natasza added. "They were molested or beaten, so they kill those who commit those atrocities. Some of us focus on certain groups in wartime. A number in the Middle East quite enjoy teaching lessons to *bacha Baz*. Vendettas against child molesters and all, you understand."

Bridget's mouth quirked. "But what about this war or whatever the hell it is? Feeding on them alone can't be enough."

"We had to get creative," Natasza answered.

Shreya nodded agreement. "We've figured out ways to combat terrorists. May I have one, Annelie?" Annelie flipped open her cigarette case and handed the Original a kretek. Smoke rose from the end as Shreya blinked; she blinked again and the glowing cherry faded. The adults gasped in awe. "All of you mistakenly believe it takes rage to do this. The only thing rage does is focus your mind. Concentration is the key." She relit the kretek and took a long drag, her eyes closing with relish. "Mmm. We've applied this *talent* to other areas. If a fuse can be lit, it can also be extinguished. We've been able to stop quite a few bombings with this idea. Imagine what we could do if we join forces."

Bridget scanned her companions who seemed mildly amused and intrigued by the Children. She next met the Original's innocent face; Shreya lifted an eyebrow at her in question as Natasza sat with a finger poised over the iPad screen. "I think I'd like to find out what we could do together."

"Brilliant! I've emailed Ajit." Natasza tapped her finger on the tablet before putting it away. "Anyone else ready to feed? I'm famished."

ॐ

"What a night!" Lucian commented, pulling his t-shirt over his head, then laying it on a chair.

Livia grinned. "No shit. Those two are... I don't even have a word for it!"

He crawled into bed next to her. "Insane? Slightly scary?" She raised an eyebrow at him. "Admit it. The horror on that drug dealer's face when Natasza bared her fangs... *ffwrch*, I almost ran away!" A deep laugh shook him. "Christ."

Shreya and Natasza had led the four on a wild tour of the underbelly of Paris, stopping to feed on human traffickers, drug dealers, and other offenders who suited their fancies. The Children lured the prey in close with tears and big eyes before latching on with preternatural strength and speed.

Livia rolled her eyes at him. "It wasn't *that* awful now!"

A corner of his mouth quirked in amusement. "You think they're endearing, don't you?" She gave him a black look. "You do! Shreya had you the moment you picked her up!"

"Maybe," she answered, her glare growing sheepish. "Shreya intrigues me. Nearly five thousand years a child! And Natasza. Natasza is… intense." She shook her head as she rolled onto her side.

Lucian spooned her, wrapping his arms around her slender waist. "That's one word for it!" He hummed. "I hope she at least finds Thad before he does something stupid."

Livia glanced back at him. "Since when did you start caring about Thad?"

"I don't care so much. Just… feel sorry for him. Finding out about Annelie that way. It's obvious he still cares for her." He squeezed her bottom.

"Shreya told us Natasza can track like a bloodhound. She'll find him—even if he doesn't want to be found." A soft yawn escaped her. "G'night. Love you."

"Love you, too." Lucian kissed her neck as she relaxed into sleep against him.

Just before he drifted off, he heard the door quietly open and close. He peeked over Livia's shoulder, meeting a plaid-pajama-clad Shreya. A bit of light reflected in her eyes as the corners of her mouth turned up softly. Lucian watched in silence as the Original gently crawled under the sheets, bringing Livia's arm then his own around her, before growing still.

Apparently, Livia isn't the only infatuated one here. This just keeps getting odder and odder, he thought, laying his head down on the pillow.

Chapter Nine

War Child

Bridget padded down the hallway, intent on listening to the goings-on in the city she called home. *There's no possibility of other visitors,* she reassured herself, glancing briefly into her study as she passed by.

She stopped in confusion and backpedalled to study the odd scene. Natasza sat with her legs tucked under her on a chaise longue, a copy of *War and Peace* open before her. Thad, dressed in a black police uniform, lay sprawled across the couch.

Natasza smiled softly, meeting Bridget's stare and raising a finger to her lips, though they both knew Thad would most likely sleep through any conversation. She set the book down as Bridget entered and sat in a nearby chair.

"You're up early," Bridget remarked, nodding toward the darkening sky.

"I've never been a good sleeper. Not even when I was human. It drives Shreya mad! She likes us to sleep like

kittens all cuddled next to one another. I just… can't."
Natasza shrugged. "I figured she'd find Livia and Lucian or
you and Morning Star to accommodate her."

A corner of Bridget's mouth pulled up as she imagined
an Original snuggling with her friends. "Must have been
Lucian and Livia."

The Child nodded, pulling her iPad from her side. "It
was." She held the tablet up, displaying the photo.

A warm feeling spread through Bridget's heart as she
viewed Shreya wrapped in Livia's and Lucian's arms. She
shook her head in amusement before turning her attention
to Thad. "Where'd you find this one?" The strong scent of
whiskey wafted to her nose as she studied the tactical
uniform Thad wore.

"I found him—completely pissed—at a bar in the
northeast of the city. He and some police officers were
celebrating a night of successful raids in Bobigny. The
Recherche Assistance Intervention Dissuasion and *Groupes
d'Intervention de la Police Nationale* have been conducting them
for the last two days. I don't know for sure, but I think he
joined them." Natasza tilted her head as she curiously
studied him. "He was excited when he saw me. Called me
over. Gave me a hug. Insisted on giving me a piggy back
ride the *entire* way back here." Her mouth opened but
closed again as she shook her head.

Bridget felt the unasked question plaguing the Child. "What? I get the feeling you want to ask something." Her lips turned up.

Natasza shifted uncomfortably and chewed her lower lip. "Well, it's… He kept asking what feeding and blood sharing is like for us Children. Lots of 'no, you know what I mean,' like he was hinting at something. I told him it probably felt the same for us as it does for you."

Bridget's lips parted as words escaped her. *I hope it's not the same for the Children,* she thought, trying not to imagine an eight-year-old child feeling the warm rush of lust and pleasure drinking blood brought adult vampires. "Um. Tell me how it feels to you, if you could."

The Child briefly pouted in confusion. "It's like eating too much candy, and then jumping on a trampoline. You know the feeling of a sugar rush?"

Bridget shook her head. "Not really. Candy was very different when I was a mortal." She squinted, trying to remember the sweets Étaín, her adoptive mother, had made. "I may have eaten too many honey cakes once," she added uncertainly.

"Oh. I forgot how old you are." She shrugged. "When we feed off a human, we feel a burst of energy and sort of light and airy at the same time. It's more intense when we share blood with one another." The Child eyed her. "How is it for you?"

"Well," Bridget began, weighing her words. "It's more… hmm…" Natazsa leaned forward expectantly. "For us it's more… sexual." *Gods, I sincerely hope she hadn't been abused before her siring.* Her stomach cartwheeled.

"Huh." Natasza sat back, contemplating the information.

Bridget inhaled a breath and asked, "Were you… you know?"

The Child smiled. "No, thankfully. The Children who were tell stories sometimes, but… The SS took me from my Polish parents as part of the *Lebensborn* program during the Second World War." She met Bridget's gaze while sweeping a hand down beside her face. "Perfect little Aryan looker, aren't I? The SS told me that my parents had died. A lovely German couple—a professor and his wife—adopted me in 1941. He taught at the Technical University of Darmstadt; she stayed at home to raise my adoptive brother, Armin, and me. All three of them died when the British firebombed the city in 1944. Shreya found me in the rubble of our home, healed my wounds, and sired me." A sigh left the girl. "I searched for my biological parents, but the SS hadn't lied. They'd shot them after taking me." A shadow passed over her sapphire eyes. "I made sure I found the one who did it." She invited Bridget into her mind.

The curious SS officer followed the sound of sobbing from the gate of his home around the corner. "Whatever is the matter, child? You shouldn't be out so late. Have you lost your way?" he asked, lowering himself to one knee beside his discovery. His hand stroked her shaking back.

Natasza huddled against the fieldstone wall, knees pulled in to her chest and hands covering her face. Glassy eyes met his as she looked up and nodded. Her bottom lip quivered as more tears rolled down her cheeks.

"Ah, come now! There's no reason to cry." He pulled a handkerchief from his uniform pocket and dabbed her cheeks. "You're safe with me. I'll find your home."

"My home, Herr?" Her eyes locked onto his. The officer's mouth gaped as the vampire slid into his mind, paralyzing him as she brought the image of her parents and house in Poland from the depths of his memories. "The home where you murdered my parents?" She flashed memories of her adoptive family's charred bodies into his brain next. "Or perhaps this home?"

A growing wet spot darkened the officer's jodhpurs as Natasza played in his head, projecting all of her worst human fears into him. "Puh... puh... please..." he stuttered, tears spilling over his face.

"I knew I could get you to beg." Natasza bared her fangs and sprang at his throat. She stood over him moments later as blood continued to slowly pump from the wound. He met her with a gurgle. "No quick death for you, Herr." Her right arm raised into the air for a salute. "Sieg Heil." She clicked her heels together then skipped off into the night.

Bridget sat back, thinking of the Child's well-deserved revenge. *Not like I never had my own. I guess it's my time again.*

"You were a child of war as well, weren't you?" Natasza asked curiously. "Morning Star's Pet took you in, and they raised you."

Bridget nodded as a memory of Étaín's kind dove-gray eyes flashed through her brain. "I suppose I was, though I've never thought of myself that way. Clan wars in Éire were nothing like what happens today. The scale of modern battles is overwhelming to think about." She puffed out her cheeks, remembering the news coverage of twentieth century wars she's seen over the years. *Trench warfare, tanks, planes, concentration camps, the atomic bomb... So many needlessly dead... And it always becomes worse...*

"Humans constantly invent more efficient ways to hurt one another." The Child frowned. "Yet, they'd call us monsters if they encountered us."

"They're always more afraid a what creeps 'round in the dark than other humans," Thad added, opening an eye. "If only they could getta look inta each others' heads like we can." He sat up and stretched, examining his uniform. "Shit. They're gonna wonder where I went. Ah, well. They'll get over it." His shoulders lifted into an abbreviated shrug. "I learned some interestin' thin's last night durin' ma adventures."

ᴈ∽ᴄ

"Abdelhamid Abaaoud," Thad stated as he pulled the tails of his shirt from his uniform trousers. "He was the ringleader of Friday's attack. A course there are tons a others plannin' shit other places, I'm sure."

"There always are," Natasza said sadly.

Weight lifted off Bridget's shoulders. Though she felt as if she should have found the perpetrator's name herself, she resisted the urge to give Thad a kiss of appreciation. "It's a start. Thank you."

Thad nodded at the acknowledgement as his fingers undid the shirt buttons. "No worries. It was a helluva time. I hadn' played cops an' cockies since I was Uncle Thaddy ta ma great-great—great?—gran'kids." He met her face. "I gotta tell ya, I don' think these cunts are gonna be easy."

Natasza tilted her head in curiosity. "With a name, Bridget doesn't have to scan the thousands of people in Paris. What could make it difficult?"

"Well," Thad started with a smirk, "there's more ta 'em than we figured. I got inta the heads ofa few last night. Somethin' wrong with 'em." He leaned forward, placing his elbows on his thighs. His steepled index fingers tapped his lips. "I hadda Pet once. Maddie was her name. Sucha beautiful woman... hair the color a black coffee... skin a light mocha."

He met Bridget and Natasza's expectant faces with distant eyes. "Yes, there's a point ta this. Maddie developed a brain tumor. Inoperable. Knew she'd get bad as time went on... asked me ta end it for her when it did. Before ya ask, she wouldn' let me heal her. An' when you're forced inta this life, ya don' force your will on others." Thad shook his head with a frustrated sigh. "Anyway, Maddie's sense a right an' wrong disappeared as the tumor grew. She became erratic. Seemed like her humanity was disappearin' at times... These cunts' brains are like hers was at the end." A finger tapped his temple. "It's a fuckin' disease what's going on in 'em."

Bridget sat back in her chair, gazing out the window in thought. After a moment she met Thad's face. "But one can still get into their heads?" she asked quietly.

"Yeah. It's a bit like fighting through a jungle a spiderwebs, but ya can."

"Good," Bridget stated, her mind working out a plan as Natasza and Thad eyed her. "That's all I need to know."

Part Two

"He who fights with monsters might take care lest he thereby become a monster."

Friedrich Nietzsche

Chapter Ten

Gonna Get Got

A clean-shaven, dark-haired, young Frenchman stood next to a lamppost by a makeshift memorial. He seemed to be quietly contemplating the masses of flowers and stuffed animals set along rue de Charonne to honor those slain four days before.

Everything that is wrong with this culture, Abdelhamid said to himself, studying the man's clothes. His eyes glimpsed the untucked cream-colored button-down shirt, dark blue blazer, and jeans and focused on the Louis Vuitton boots the man wore. *Western decadence. I'm certain they cost as much as my rent. Huh! Greed at its worst.*

The Frenchman turned and acknowledged him with a nod. Their gazes locked, but the look in the stranger's hazel eyes was unreadable.

He knows. Abdelhamid's chest tightened. *Shut up, you fool! How could he? You are nothing but another faceless immigrant to him.* He paused, closing his eyes and pretending to say a prayer.

When he opened his eyes, the stranger was still regarding him nonchalantly. He glanced around quickly, his pulse racing. *You shouldn't be out in this atmosphere! They're looking at all of us that way! No, no. That's what we want—they need to fear us all. Show their true colors. Bring others to our cause.*

The stranger smirked, a dark eyebrow rising as a Gallic shrug lifted his shoulders. He slid his hands into his pants' pockets and slowly started down the sidewalk.

Abdelhamid tried to follow with his gaze but quickly lost him. *The crowd is large. He didn't just disappear,* he assured himself with a relieved sigh. He turned in the opposite direction and headed for Saint-Denis.

An hour later Abdelhamid stopped short in front of the block of flats. The dark-haired stranger leaned against the side of the building, arms crossed on his chest. A corner of his mouth quirked as he met Abdelhamid's face.

He steeled himself and approached the young Frenchman, wanting to know who he was and why he followed him. But the Frenchman *did* disappear before his eyes this time. An icy wave chilled Abdelhamid as he heard a deep voice say, "She'll be there every step you take."

༄•༄

A long breath left Bridget's lips. She could feel the wool of Bastien's jacket on her cheek and smell his cologne as she let his image slip from her mind. His smiling face calmed her as it faded.

She had started something she looked forward to finishing. *How had Thad put it? Somebody's gonna get got.*

ح‍مك‍د

Livia suppressed the yawn threatening to crack her jaw as a look of peace spread over Bridget's tired face. She studied the hollows under her friend's eyes with worry. Bridget had kept herself awake a day and a half since Thad brought her the information from the raids. The rest of them sat with her in turn for support.

Bridget met her gaze with a weak smile. "I've told you all, you don't have to sit with me. I'm fine." She laughed quietly as one of Livia's eyebrows lifted in doubt. "Really. I'm a little tired, but I'll make it."

"If you say so," Livia answered, returning the smile as a thought passed through her mind. "Out of curiosity, would Bastien have minded what you're doing? Using his image to mentally torment someone, even if the person deserves it?"

An uncomfortable look passed over the Elder's features. "Remember your opinion of the people carrying out these attacks?" Livia nodded. "Well… Bastien wasn't exactly a fan of Islam as a whole. There were times I was hard-pressed to keep him quiet when we walked near a Middle-Easterner wearing too much cologne or perfume on the street."

Livia snorted in amusement. "Sorry, I shouldn't laugh at that." A twinge of guilt hit her while she fought to suppress a giggle. "Not really appropriate to laugh at another's prejudices, is it?"

"Trust me, I'm just as bad as you. I did more than once. One's sense of humor tends to darken and very little offends after nearly seventeen hundred years." A wide grin split Bridget's face. "He never would have done anything to a person of their religion—or any other—he just… let's say, he had reasons for his dislike." She brought her legs up onto her chair and tucked them under her. "He grew up next door to a Muslim family in Lisieux and used to play with their daughter, who was the same age. When they got to be around nine or ten, her older brother caught them kissing. I'm sure you can imagine how that went over."

"Like the *Hindenburg*?"

Bridget tilted her head side to side, weighing the comparison. "Possibly worse. The girl's father sent her away to her grandparents in Saudi Arabia."

A chill ran through Livia as she thought about the stories she'd read about women growing up under Shari'a Law.

"Bastien's family never heard what happened to her, but, once he got older, he figured it wasn't good. Things went downhill from there, though." She grunted. "It escalated that Christmas. The girl's family loudly commented on their decorations being 'disgusting.' Bastien's father replied they should move back to their homeland if they didn't like living in a Catholic nation. Not quite helpful to the situation. Next, they called the police, making a noise complaint when Bastien's family sang carols Christmas Eve."

Livia felt the disgust on her face. "All because of a kiss between innocent children?"

"Basically. Finally, a couple weeks into the new year, the girl's older brother attacked Bastien on his way home from school. His father had a little word with their father after that... Bastien never found out what his dad said, but the girl's family left Lisieux a month later." Bridget shrugged. "Those experiences stayed with him."

"How could they not? To not only lose a friend but to be treated as a criminal by her family because of their innocence." To Livia's annoyance, the yawn finally escaped past her lips. She watched the corners of Bridget's mouth fight to stay down as Bridget slid from her chair to join her on the couch.

"If you refuse to leave me, sleep here while I do my thing," she said, pulling Livia into her arms. "You don't have to be awake to support me."

Livia guiltily let sleep take over as Bridget stroked her hair.

৯৵৶

"Did anyone see us?" Abdelhamid demanded of Hasna as they entered the building. He roughly pulled her through the entryway, glancing at the rue du Corbillon, as she grunted her displeasure. The people passing by seemed disinterested in them.

Hasna frowned at him, rubbing her arm. "No. Stop being paranoid. What's gotten into you?"

"I—nothing." She would think him mad if he told her about the Frenchman who had followed him and disappeared the day before. *The hazel eyes… what had been the look? Knowing? Disgust? Hatred?* He ignored the churning of his stomach and dragged her up the stairs.

Later that evening when Abdelhamid saw the Frenchman staring up at his window, he somehow knew it would be soon.

৵৽৽

It had started early that morning. November eighteenth. Four-twenty a.m. by the clock on the wall of the flat. Heavy footsteps pounded up the steps to the second floor. Angry voices shouted commands. But they'd managed to barricade themselves in after repelling the attack. The explosives the police used were no match for the armored door. Hasna and Chakib shot him cocky glances, but Abdelhamid knew this would be the end. The Frenchman was a portent.

They heard the reinforcements arrive: French military followed by ambulances followed by helicopters followed by more police.

How much time has passed? Minutes? Hours? Days? Abdelhamid wondered, adrenaline making him shake. The shouting and whirring of the blades drove him mad. He longed for it to be over as he glanced at his accomplices. *They still believe this is glorious death. Do I?*

The gunfire finally came three hours after the ordeal began. Staccato *crack-crack-cracks* reverberated through the building.

Abdelhamid saw Chakib run toward the door and knew what he meant to do before the words "Allahu Akbar" came out of his mouth. He and Hasna cowered behind the rolling shield they'd constructed days earlier as Chakib's explosives detonated. His ears rang.

Hasna ran to the back of the flat as the police streamed through the door.

Abdelhamid fired his pistol at the police as bullets flew in his direction. Scores of fiery stings hit him as an officer lobbed a grenade in his direction. He threw himself down, but it didn't matter. White hot agony tore through his body before he hit the floor.

Every part of him burned as he felt blood ooze from the shrapnel wounds. *Not much longer. The pain can't last long. I'll pass out before—.* His eyes opened into slits as a hand touched his head.

The dark-haired Frenchman, still dressed as he'd been the day before, sat cross-legged at his side, studying him

with that smirk. Police ran in all directions behind him, but
he didn't seem to care. And they didn't seem to notice the
stranger. "How does it feel, Abdelhamid? Torn to shreds?"
the man's bass voice asked. "I can't remember much from
the AK-47 shot, but I did get it right through my heart. A
quicker death than you'll get. A more peaceful one as well. I
died almost instantly, in the arms of the woman I love,
knowing her love." He sighed, his hazel eyes darkening.
"You, however, will die knowing her hate. She will stay in
you, keeping you conscious, making you *feel* all of this until
your last heartbeat."

⤳•⤳

Every nerve in Bridget's body throbbed from the effort
it took to hang onto Abdelhamid Abaaoud's mind until his
last breath. Any energy she had left drained from her
immediately, leaving her heart and mind empty. She pulled
her knees into her chest and bowed her head into them as
silent sobs shook her. "It's done. It's done. Done… fuck…"

⤳•⤳

Bridget's exhaustion washed over Lucian as he watched
her curl herself into a quivering ball next to him on the
couch. He hesitated, not sure if his touch would startle her,
then petted her tangled hair.

Her head slowly rose. "It's done." She shuddered
violently.

Lucian let his gaze wander over his sire's face, wondering if he had ever seen her look so tired. Dark circles surrounded her teary eyes. Her cheeks were gaunt and her skin dull. He wrapped his arms around her and pulled her onto his lap.

"Go ahead and say it," she said with a heavy exhalation.

He lifted an eyebrow. "Say what?"

A weak *huh* escaped her. "That I look like shit. I can always count on you to tell me the truth."

"Well..." Lucian returned the laugh without enthusiasm. "You do look like shite. You've been awake for days. I don't care how powerful you are, you should've slept."

Bridget glanced up at him. "I've done this before. Centuries ago. Though not to torture anyone." A yawn spread her mouth wide as she laid her head back on his shoulder.

He pursed his lips as he tried to remember. They had spent centuries living and traveling the world together before falling out. "Did you? I don't recall you ever doing such a thing."

"Mmmm... you wouldn't remember. It was just before I sired you." Her body relaxed against him. "When I found you at your manor, you stopped breathing as I picked you up. I gave you my blood, but you didn't wake up for days. I had promised Tesni, that if anything happened to her, I would protect you and love you as much as she did. If you had died, my vow would have been broken."

Lucian's heart gave a painful thump. Not knowing about Bridget's friendship with Tesni had destroyed their relationship once. But his sire's confession didn't raise his ire this time. He swallowed the lump growing in his throat and offered his wrist to Bridget. "You need to drink and rest," he ordered.

As her fangs slid into his skin, he eased them down to lie on the couch. The distance his sire went for the people she loved suddenly amazed him. "How's that old song of yours go?" He closed his eyes, remembering as he changed certain words to fit Bridget. *"Kissed by the flames, you are, my love, take my hand and follow. We'll conquer all we see, my love. And bring life to the fire. Cross this river with me, my copper-haired child…"*

Chapter Eleven

Vampires on a Plane

Cassandra Monroe looked towards the interview room door as it opened and closed quietly. A woman wearing khaki slacks and a blue blouse gave her a warm smile as she extended her hand.

"I'm Agent Moss. It's a pleasure to meet you, despite the circumstances, Miss Monroe."

"Please, call me Cassie Lynn. It would make me a helluva lot more comfortable being here!" She chewed the inside of her cheek.

"Cassie Lynn it is then. I'm going to be recording this interview, if that's all right?" she asked, heading over to the corner of the room as Cassie Lynn nodded. Agent Moss clicked on the camera, then sat down across the table. "Agent Sinead Moss. Interview with Cassandra 'Cassie Lynn' Monroe, Flight 304 eyewitness." Agent Moss's face softened. "We're going to start with a few questions about you and then move onto what you experienced on the plane. Have you had any prior interaction with law enforcement of any kind?"

The younger woman grinned proudly. "My dad was a Pennsylvania State trooper until he retired last year. You could say I've had *a lot* of prior interaction." Her face fell. "Shit! He and Mama are probably freaking out. I should have called them." Helplessness crossed her face.

"I'm sure they'll understand. Announcements were made that everyone on board arrived here in Pittsburgh safely. Besides, this won't take…" The agent trailed off as she noticed dried blood on Cassie Lynn's sweater. "Were you injured? Do you need an EMT?"

Cassie Lynn pulled the hem away from her lap. The stain darkened a large patch on the right side; a small slice opening the fabric didn't register in her mind. She studied it, her light brows knitting together. "N-no. I don't think I was. It must be someone else's." A shoulder lifted as she released the hem.

The agent dipped her head. "As long as you're okay, we'll continue. All I need you to do now is tell me what happened on the flight. Be as detailed as you can. Take your time. We're in no rush."

A whoosh of air left Cassie Lynn's lungs. "Well, I was in London visiting my cousin. We decided to visit Paris my last weekend, and I changed my return flight to leave from Charles de Gaulle…"

❧❧

Two Nights Earlier in Paris

Lucian stared longingly at Livia as she hugged Bridget. Every time they parted ways—no matter how short the duration—he found himself doing the same thing: memorizing each detail of her. He inhaled deeply. *Vanilla and amaretto,* his brain mused, his mouth watering at the thought of her blood. *Her favorite corset lacing up her curves. That glorious ar—*

Thad's hand coming to rest on his shoulder snapped him out of the reverie. "C'mon, mate. It won' be forever."

Lucian smirked at the reason he and Livia would be apart.

"The five of us will head to the States," Shreya announced to Lucian, Livia, Annelie, and Thad after Bridget told them of the ringleader's death. "Natasza will stay with Bridget. They can focus on targets over here: airports and train stations. We'll leave in a few days' time."

Thad clapped his hands together and gave them a rub. "So... who's gonna carry me?"

The others turned to him in confusion.

"Oh. That's right," Annelie mumbled, realization in her words. "You can't fly."

Thad glanced her way briefly before averting his eyes. His week-long avoidance of Annelie made it clear he wouldn't soon forgive her past. "Can' fly. Unfortunate side effect of a bat-shit insane Aborigine decidin' ta sire twenty a us inna shot. Never got tha' ability. So who's gonna carry me?" He surveyed the group with a cocky grin, his gaze landing on Livia.

Natasza piped up before Thad could get his obvious thought out. "Maybe you and Lucian should take a plane over. It wouldn't hurt to have some of us on them. Just in case. You could get a red-eye flight."

Thad's eyes narrowed into slits as his head tilted down toward the Child. "Cock block," he muttered.

Natasza's jaw gaped in confusion as she looked up at him.

"Are you *sure* you'll be fine without us?" Livia asked Bridget for the third time, bringing Lucian's attention back to her.

Shreya took Livia's hand. "She'll be well taken care of, I assure you. Natasza has never let me down."

Bridget tightly embraced Livia before kissing her. "I'll be fine, I promise. The worst is over for me... for the most part." Her arms wrapped around Annelie next. "Let me know when you get there." She bade farewell to the Original last. "Thank you for your help. I never imagined meeting you... especially this way."

A knowing smile graced the girl's young face. "It will be hard to keep me away, now that I know all of you." Her tiny arms squeezed the other vampire.

Lucian waited for Livia to finish her goodbyes, continuing his survey of her. "Be careful," he said as she came to a stop in front of him.

Livia took his hands in hers. "I've made this flight hundreds of times now. You're the one who's going to be on a plane full of humans." She rose onto her toes to get closer to his ear. "With Thad," she whispered playfully.

"Don't remind me! Better than one of us carrying him across the Atlantic though." An exaggerated groan left his throat. "I'm going to miss you." He brought his lips to hers.

She returned the kiss softly, lingering a moment before meeting his eyes. "At least it won't be long this time."

"That's no consolation."

"I know." Livia ran her fingers through his hair. "I love you." She rubbed her face against his.

"I love you, too," he replied as she turned to join Annelie and Shreya. His stomach tightened as he watched them leave, Shreya taking both Annelie's and Livia's hands.

༽ঌ

Lucian unlatched his seatbelt as soon as the light went off, eased the roomy seat back, and stretched out his legs. *I was worried, but nine hours like this can't be too awful.* He turned up his iPod and glanced around the cabin of the Air France jet. Though most of the seats were taken, they had a front row of four to themselves in the premium economy class— not first class, but Thad had been thinking ahead. By the overall number of people he'd seen board the other cabins, it seemed red-eye flights were fairly popular.

A tug at his t-shirt sleeve pulled him out of a doze. He lazily turned his head toward Thad and popped out his earbuds. "Hmm?"

"Uh, mate, Livia *did* already make it ta the States, righ'?" Thad glanced over his shoulder, though he couldn't see behind him.

"Yeah, why—shite…"

A young woman with long honey-blond hair and big dark blue eyes holding a tattered copy of *Vanilla Blood* appeared behind Thad. She bit her bottom lip nervously before offering a small grin.

That's why, Thad replied directly into Lucian's brain.

"Hi, um, I'm really sorry to bother you, but I saw you on my way back to my seat and… You're Lucian Llewellyn, aren't you?" She hugged the novel to her.

Ffwrch, er, fuck. That's Livia's daughter. Livia gave her up for adoption when she was born, he silently told his companion, studying the young woman before him, her mother's doppelgänger.

Oooh, a daughter… Thad smiled wide as he turned.

Lucian inhaled deeply, mentally preparing himself to face both the young woman and Thad's inevitable flirting with her. "It's no bother. That's me." Her excited energy washed over him as he confirmed his identity. "Have a seat, um… what's your name?" *Not that I don't already know it.* He motioned to an empty one between Thad and him.

"Cassie Lynn." She slid down in the seat next to Thad and looked from him to Thad with glee. "I never thought I'd *ever* get this close to one of my favorite authors!" Her eyes roamed over Lucian's jeans, t-shirt, and Doc Martens. "I figured you didn't wear velvet, satin, and lace all the time, but I didn't think you'd be so down-to-earth."

Thad offered his hand to her. "Thad Boyd, Lucian's personal assistant." Lucian rolled his eyes "Nice ta meet ya."

"What beautiful accents you both have!"

"You're definitely your mother's daughter," Lucian mumbled as quietly as he could.

"Aren' ya a bit young ta be reading Lucian's books?" Thad flashed his white teeth flirtatiously. "I thought people your age preferred glitterin' vampires."

Cassie Lynn shook her head, rolling her eyes. "That shit? Vampires going to high school and hooking up with teenagers? *Serious* issues there! Perverts really. I could never stomach those books and the carbon copies they caused. No… I cut my teeth on *Carmilla* and *Dracula*, snuck Anne Rice and him under my sheets. Your books kept true to legends, even if the vampires were out in the open. You were the reason for my goth phase in high school!" She relaxed back in the seat with a soft laugh and held *Vanilla Blood* up in front of her. "You can probably tell this one is my favorite. I must've read it a dozen times. I always felt a connection to Janie and Nate."

They're based off the mother and uncle you never met... so... Lucian fought to keep the thought in his head with an uncomfortable smile.

"Have I said something wrong? I'm sorry... I can be such a spazz," Cassie Lynn apologized, her face falling.

"God, no! Lucian's just not usedta meetin' fans anymore! Are ya, mate?"

An encouraging look from Thad met him. "Thad's right. I stay a recluse nowadays." He shot the other vampire a silent thanks. "Keeps the mystery alive and all. I love your love of my books. Here, let me sign it for you."

"I can't thank you enough." Relief spread over the young woman's features as she handed the paperback to him like a sacred tome. "Wou-would you mind if I asked you something about the book?"

An eyebrow raised in curiosity as he pulled out a pen. "I suppose not..." Lucian answered, opening the cover to autograph the title page. "Go for it."

"I always wondered about the dedication. Who was Evan?"

The pen stopped halfway to the page as breath caught in his throat. His heart lurched. *Of course it would be that question...*

Chapter Twelve

Mile-High Fight Club

Lucian pushed the service button. "Could we have another round of wine, *s'il vous plâit?*" He gazed innocently up at the sleepy stewardess.

"Oui. But don't blame me if you all have *les gueules de bois* in the morning," the woman joked, grinning and tapping her temple lightly. She disappeared down the aisle.

It had taken quite a bit of persuading to get the first three small bottles of wine, but he, Thad, and Cassie Lynn had kept their promise to be as quiet as humanly possible while other passengers slept.

Lucian's jaw dropped as he turned back to his companions. *Looks like she really has her mother's affinity toward accents.* Cassie Lynn's and Thad's mouths pressed into one another, soft moans escaping. He shook his head and cleared his throat. *Talk about pervy vampires. She's only nineteen, Thad... And Livia will kill you if she finds out.*

Cassie Lynn released the kiss first, her cheeks flushed. She finished the wine in her glass, biting her bottom lip nervously.

Sorry, mate... It jus' sorta happened... Thad avoided Lucian's gaze as the stewardess returned with more chardonnay.

Lucian passed the bottles down, then watched the young woman fill her glass and take a long sip.

"So," Cassie Lynn started, seemingly more composed, "you never made amends with Evan before he died. I'm so sorry. My God, your poor wi—"

"Monsieur, I *must insist* you return to your seat! I *cannot* allow you to—"

The three of them turned as the flight attendant hit the nearest row with an *oomph.*

Other passengers, roused from sleep, peeked over seats and stood up as four armed men made their way up the aisle.

Cassie Lynn's eyes widened as Thad and Lucian exchanged glances.

"There goes our good time, mate." Thad unscrewed the top of the small bottle and drank it in one gulp.

☙❧

"Whatever you do, don't let them know you're an American," Lucian whispered to Cassie Lynn, leaning in close.

Though tears glazed her eyes, she gave him a smile. "*Moi? Américaine? Non. Je suis française,*" she replied with a perfect accent.

"Clever girl," Lucian said as the crying and whispered prayers of other passengers met his ears. "You'll be safe." He squeezed her hand and glanced up at one of the men. *She'd better be.* His stomach twisted as he imagined having to tell Livia if something bad happened to the only child she'd ever have. "I promise."

Cassie Lynn trembled but returned the squeeze.

"Shut the *fuck* up!" One of the hijackers turned to them, waving his pistol.

Fake, Thad stated silently to Lucian. *The guns are fake. Do like Shreya taught us an' see.*

Lucian focused on the gun and remembered the Original's instructions: "*Imagine the inner workings of a gun, a bomb… anything, and destroy what ignites it, be it a firing pin or a spark.*" A corner of his mouth quirked up. *Toy guns with the orange caps removed.* He tried to slip into the terrorist's mind, but a muddled wall met him. Imagining himself a machete slicing through jungle vines, he pushed through. *Ahh… that's your game! Nothing like an early morning tragedy to instill fear in the masses. Not putting us in the Atlantic today, arseholes!*

Two of the armed men stormed to the front; screams floated back as more passengers realized they sat on a hijacked plane. The other men took places at the heads of the aisles, plastic rifles positioned across their chests. Loud pounding echoed throughout the plane as the first two men tried to force their way into the cockpit.

The reek of shite, piss, vomit, and sweat assaulted Lucian's nostrils. *Primal fear. None of these people should have to experience it.* He glanced over at Cassie Lynn, who hugged her knees to her chest; she bowed her head and shook with muffled sobs as Thad rubbed her back distractedly.

"S'il vous plâit, tout le monde, restez calme." The flight attendant who had tried to stop the hijackers rose unsteadily to her feet. "Everyone, please remain cal—" The butt of a rifle met her stomach, bringing her to the floor once again.

"Cunt," Thad mumbled. His head snapped to the side as he, too, was introduced to a fake AK-47; blood oozed from his forehead. He turned to Lucian, a deadly black look in his chocolate diamond eyes. *I've hadda 'bout enough a this, mate. I'll get this cockie, ya get tha' one.*

Lucian nodded, the corners of his mouth pulling up as adrenaline surged through him. *One… two… three.* They rose in unison, pushing the hijackers into the restroom area behind them to the startled cries and gasps of the men and their fellow passengers.

The hijacker grunted as Lucian pinned him facedown, locking the man's arm behind him. He fought to turn his head and sneered up at his captor. "Get off, you filth! You can't stop us! You'll all die to——"

Lucian twisted the captured limb until he heard the muffled crack of breaking bones. *You're never going to use that arm again.* He waited for the pained howl to stop, then leaned in close to the hijacker's ear. "Not today we're not." With a quick jerk, he pulled the man's belt off, tearing through the double-D buckle like paper. A moment later, much to the hijacker's protests, the vampire had him hog-tied, gagged with his own shirt, and shoved into a restroom.

Taking a deep breath and resisting the urge to laugh, Lucian turned to Thad and his adversary. *Hmmm… slightly different approach: letting the arsehole think he's winning.* Thad had let the hijacker straddle him on the floor as they struggled for the plastic firearm, but Lucian could see the feral look in his companion's eyes. *A cat playing with a mouse. Crazy bastard.*

A wicked grin split Thad's face as he finally asserted his dominance. The hijacker landed at Lucian's feet, dazed. Thad pounced on top of him, fangs bared.

Lucian glanced up, meeting the curious faces of Cassie Lynn and two other passengers. "Thad! *Thad!*"

"*What?*" Thad's chest heaved as he looked up and followed Lucian's gaze. *Oh, righ', mate. No vampin' out,* he silently replied. His fist squarely met the hijacker's face with a loud crunch, the recipient growing still. "Takes care a him fora while." Raising to his feet, he grabbed the faux AK-47 and snapped it in two over his thigh. "Plastic."

"Holy…" Cassie Lynn muttered, her jaw going slack. "You two are fucking insane."

Thad gently put his hands on her shoulders. "Listen ta me: Go back ta the seat. Stay there. *Stay safe.*" He met the passengers' faces. "All a ya. *Go.*"

She swallowed hard, glancing from Thad to Lucian, then nodded and left. The others followed wordlessly.

☜☞

"Uh… thanks for that," Thad whispered, leaning in towards Lucian. "Fangs probably'd be a bad idea on a plane fulla people."

Lucian chuckled. "Probably so." He gathered up the unconscious attacker and shoved him into another restroom. "We should be getting more company so—"

Passengers' panicked screams and the guttural war cries of the approaching terrorists interrupted him. He and Thad positioned themselves at the end of the aisles, ready to take one apiece.

"They make this too easy," Thad muttered.

As Lucian watched his opponent approach, in his peripheral, he noticed Thad sidestep and raise an arm just as the hijacker reached him. The arm met the man directly in his throat, and he fell backwards and slid, sputtering in surprise.

Lucian didn't have time to enjoy the scene as his opponent reached him the moment Thad's attacker fell. He stopped the hijacker with a gentle palm to the chin and swept the man's legs from under him at the ankle, grabbing the hijacker's foot as it came up into the air.

"How dare you! You'll all pay for this! You've brought death to everyone on this plane!" The dangling man struggled to grab his captor. "Let me *go*!"

"Let you go?" The vampire eased his grip, his prisoner's face nearly touching the floor as he dropped a foot before Lucian lifted him up higher.

"You—I will end you."

Lucian straightened up, unbuckled his belt, and pulled it from the denim loops. "I'm really sick of you." He doubled the metal-grommeted leather, then started cracking it over his captive's backside. The sound brought wicked pleasure to his face. "You know what I'm thinking? If your mother had done this when you were a child, we'd have fewer issues here." A metal grommet ripped through the khaki fabric of the hijacker's pants. The hijacker wept, another lash meeting his bare skin.

"An' here I thought I got joy outta tha' clotheslinin'!"

Lucian turned—the terrorist's head banging against the wall—to find Thad laughing at him. "I couldn't let you have all the fun, could I?" His arm raised high and his fingers opened, dropping the man face-first to the floor. He slid his belt back on as the fragrance of vanilla wafted to his nostrils. "That's odd…"

"They aren't your saviors! You will all die today! She is just the beginning!"

"Shit!"

Thad and Lucian rushed around the dividing wall, finding Cassie Lynn slumped against the other side, balled up and clutching her side. Thad knelt beside her as the hijacker opened his coat, revealing a chest-full of explosives. The man held an old cellphone high above his head, a victorious look on his face.

They're real unfortunately. Thad glanced up at Lucian. *Migh' be better if we do it together. You take the phone, I'll get the rest.*

To the sobs, prayers, and wails of the plane's passengers, Lucian infiltrated the cellphone's inner workings. *Tiny, green, and complicated. There you are, microprocessor!* The technology pushed against his efforts but broke a second later. *So simple, yet I never realized I could do it.*

"Prepare for your ends!" The hijacker pushed a button on the mobile phone. Defeat and confusion washed over his features before he fled towards the back of the Boeing 777.

Lucian knelt beside Cassie Lynn, kissing her ashen forehead. "It *will* be all right. *You will* be all right, I promise." Her glassy eyes met his, a pained squeak answering him.

"Got her good a few times... She's fadin'..." Thad swallowed hard.

"Help her. I'll take care of that one." Lucian stood then strode down the aisle in pursuit.

৵৵

Lucian barely noticed the gazes of his fellow passengers —some panicked, some disbelieving—as he pursued his quarry down the aisle. Cassie Lynn's pained face and the thought of Livia losing the girl narrowed his vision as adrenaline sped through his limbs.

The hijacker turned to face him, waving a black knife as the vampire reached the stern of the plane. "Don't come any closer! Just let me go, or I'll take you out like I did the little bitch." He eyed the emergency doors.

"Little bitch? Because... I wasn't annoyed with you enough?" Lucian lunged just as the man slashed at him. The blade sliced through his forearm, nearly reaching bone. *Composite plastic. That's a new feeling.* He smirked at the man while the itchy tingle of muscle and flesh knitting together spread to his fingers. "Do it again," the vampire whispered, closing the distance between them. Another burning slash met his upper arm, then the blade slid between his ribs, sticking there.

"What the fuck?" Fear and confusion mingled in the terrorist's eyes. His mouth worked like that of a fish out of water. *"What are you?"*

97

Lucian pulled the knife from his side with one hand while his other grabbed the terrorist by the shirt, lifting him off his feet and pinning him to the wall. He leaned in close, a rush of bloodlust baring his fangs. "Any guesses?"

Jumbled words resembling a prayer escaped the hijacker's lips as he clawed at Lucian's arm. The ammonia reek of piss filled the small space. *"Demon."*

"It all depends, doesn't it?" Lucian asked, lips to the man's ear. "I was here for a ride to the States. You boarded to kill people. Who's worse?" He slipped the blade through skin, puncturing the man's carotid artery and pulled it free, blood spraying his face. His mouth found the wound a second later, aiding the process.

He let the hijacker drop to the floor, kicked him in the ribs, then wiped his mouth before heading back towards his cabin. *You tasted like shite.*

❧

Lucian's feet stopped moving before his brain registered the scene in front of him. His stomach dropped and his knees buckled, adrenaline draining from him. Thad sat cradling Cassie Lynn in his lap, his stare distant as he petted her tangled hair; Cassie Lynn's eyes were closed and her face and body relaxed against Thad's chest.

"N-no…" Blood rushed through his ears. *Livia… What the hell am I going to say?* He reached out to touch Cassie Lynn.

"Huh?" Thad shook his head, meeting Lucian's face. "Nah. She-she's fine." He gave a lopsided grin, then quickly ran his tongue over an exposed fang. *I'm no Prince Charmin', but a lil' kiss from me worked.* A shudder ran through him. *Firs' time I healed someone who was that close ta dyin'… Nervewrackin', especially knowin' the stakes.*

Lucian nodded and sat down, propping himself up against the row of seats. His head fell back in exhaustion. "I'm never flying commercial again."

Thad glanced at him and chuckled. "Migh' wanna wipe your face, mate… And I hope tha' wasn' your favorite shirt."

He ran his hands down his cheeks and looked. "Shite. Sid Vicious gave me this shirt…"

Chapter Thirteen

Chance Encounters

"...Thad told me and the others to go back to our seats..." Cassie Lynn's brow furrowed as she thought. "Then things get a little hazy. I must've fainted."

Agent Moss nodded. "It's understandable if you did. The stress, the fear."

The young woman chewed her lower lip uncomfortably. "Yeah, I... I guess. A stewardess woke me up later. Lucian and Thad had been the first to get off the plane when we landed, she told me, because of how they'd saved us. They'd asked her to take care of me." She fished a well-worn book out of her purse and grinned. "Lucian made sure I didn't lose this... though, I think, there may be some blood on it... I suppose that's acceptable for a vampire novel... I'm hoping to find him and Thad and thank them..."

৵৽

Livia ran her trembling fingers over Lucian's chest, shaking her head as she reached the knife hole. "This was your favorite shirt."

Lucian gently caught her hand and held it to his heart, a corner of his mouth lifting at the feel of her skin on his. "Yeah… we'll call it a sacrifice for the good of the many." He studied the faraway look in her eyes. "Are you all right?"

A tremor ran through her. "Cassie Lynn wasn't supposed to be on that flight."

He pulled her into him, petting her hair. "I know. But she's safe now. Thad healed her; she slept like a baby the rest of the flight. And she won't remember being stabbed or the pain or the fear of it—a glorious side effect of the Blood on a human."

"I know…"

Lucian tilted her face up and kissed her forehead. "Then there's no need to overthink it, is there?" He lifted an eyebrow at her; her head shook in response. "We'd better go. Dawn's coming. Thad's going to meet us in Belle Hollow." One hand slid to the small of Livia's back as the other reached for his carry-on. "I need about a week of you all to myself before he gets there." An image of them lying nude under the sheets of her four-poster bed rolled through his tired mind, making him purr.

Livia laughed softly as they started for the exit. "If only we had—"

"Lucian! Wait! Please! Lucian!"

≈∽≈

Livia's breath hitched and her heart skipped a beat as she turned to see Cassie Lynn running towards them. Her stomach twisted as her eyes glided over the dried blood on the young woman's sweater. *So close to losing her.* She fumbled for Lucian's fingers, adrenaline flooding her veins; he squeezed her hand, a look of reassurance in his sterling eyes.

A breathless Cassie Lynn caught up to them. "Oh… I was *so* afraid I wouldn't be able to find you!" She glanced from Lucian to Livia and back, joy lighting up her face even though tears glazed her dark blue eyes. "I wanted to thank you for… everything." She wrapped her arms around Lucian.

He looked down at Cassie Lynn then at Livia before returning the young woman's embrace. "It was nothing… really, Cassie Lynn."

Warmth replaced Livia's nervousness as she studied them. *How many times have I thought about this? Lucian and I being humans, raising a family. How he would have taken care of her like his own.* The young woman's voice brought her back to the present.

"Saving a plane full of people? Nothing, huh? You *are* crazy!" Cassie Lynn exhaled as she released the hug, turning and grasping Livia's hands in hers. "You're Livia

Hart… I've been following The Bard's Immortal Players forever." Her gaze roamed over Livia's face. "People always say we look so much alike, and I see it now—we could be sisters! Weird, huh?"

Just breathe, Lucian told her silently.

Livia nodded, enjoying the feel of Cassie Lynn's palms in hers. *I wish I could have done this when you were a child.* Her thumbs ran softly over her daughter's knuckles. "We do look amazingly alike." She smiled, allowing herself to relax.

"You're the reason I decided to get into theatre. Next year, I start at Juilliard for Fine Arts." Cassie Lynn's face grew somber. "Lucian told me about the brother you lost. I-I'm so sorry." Her eyes wandered over Livia's left forearm, then she embraced Livia gently.

Livia squeezed her eyes shut, knowing Lucian had explained *Vanilla Blood's* dedication to her. Pushing a pang of longing for Evan and the woman in front of her down, she returned the hug. She inhaled deeply, memorizing the fragrance of her daughter's hair and skin. "Thank you, Cassie Lynn." Her mind wandered, more dreams of what could have been playing in her mind.

Cassie Lynn looked around, biting her lip. "I was hoping to thank Thad as well."

"He's… um… already gone ahead of us," Lucian told her, breaking Livia from her reverie. "But I'll make sure he knows you wanted to talk to him."

Livia fought to keep her eyes from narrowing as she noticed Cassie Lynn's eyes grow dreamy.

"Oh… shit… Yeah. Please make sure he knows." She tucked a lock of honey-blond hair behind her ear and motioned behind her. "I'd better get back to my parents. Thank you again, Lucian. It was wonderful meeting you, Livia." Cassie Lynn turned to wave as she left them.

Livia watched until the young woman disappeared into the crowd, then looked up at Lucian, who avoided her face. "Did Thad and my daughter…?"

He tilted his head side to side as he weighed his words. "Hmmm… um, they'd a bit of a *cwtsh*… She may have inherited your love of accents." His hand moved once again to the small of her back as they moved toward the doors.

❧◦❧

"Well, took some work, but I don' think we have ta worry! The cockies are—" Thad stopped when he noticed Livia's face. "Ah, shit." He glanced up at Lucian, his shoulders drooping. "How'd she find out?"

Lucian hummed deep in his throat. "Cassie Lynn may've come to find us at the airport. It was obvious from the look in her eyes when she asked where you were."

"Shit… A hundred fifty-eight years an' this is how it ends."

Annelie and Shreya glanced at one another in confusion as Livia silently approached Thad.

"Can ya at least make it quick an' painless?" Thad begged, his eyes finally meeting the other vampire's.

"Shut up, Thad," Livia answered, the corners of her mouth lifting in amusement. "I'm not going to hurt you. Just… relax." She slid gently into his mind.

Thad watched Lucian pursue the hijacker as Cassie Lynn's head dropped against his chest. "No, no, no." He took her face in his hands. "Look at me. Wake up!"

Her eyes opened slowly, meeting his. "Thad? I'm so cold." She gasped, her body shuddering. "I'm going to die."

A ball of ice pinballed in his stomach as her fear hit him, but he forced his mouth into a small smile. "Nah, you're fine, I promise. Just a scratch." He listened to her labored breathing and weakening heartbeat as he glanced around the cabin, meeting terrified and curious faces. How the hell am I gonna do this with everyone watchin'?

"No, it's not. My arm's off." A sigh left her as her eyelids slid down.

Shit, shit shit! *He winced as he bit a chunk from his tongue and sealed his lips over hers, carefully sliding his injured tongue into her mouth. A minute later, his mouth left hers and he stared down at her ashen face.* Oh, God, it didn't work. *His heart lurched as he pulled her still body into his lap, dread pressing down on his chest.*

Thad started as Cassie Lynn's back arched against him and she pulled in a deep breath. She looked up at him in confusion. "What happened?"

Relief and exhaustion washed over him as he petted her hair. "Not a thin'. Go ta sleep." He kissed her temple.

She nodded her head as she relaxed against him.

He leaned back against the wall, shutting out the voices around him in favor of his own thoughts.

With his brow furrowed, Thad met Livia's eyes as she slid from his memories. "Ya coulda jus' asked."

Livia pursed her lips, ashamed of herself for invading his mind without permission. "You're right... I-I'm sorry." She softly took his cheeks in her hands, moving his face down to hers to kiss his forehead. "Thank you for saving her."

Thad inclined his head as she released his face.

Livia inhaled deeply, turning Cassie Lynn's and Thad's fear from his memory over in her mind. The corners of her mouth rose in a small, dark smile as she made for the door. *Time to meet our guests.*

Chapter Fourteen

Fighting Monsters

Livia surveyed the three unconscious men before her, pouting. *How sad I don't get to meet the one who stabbed Cassie Lynn. Just rotting away in a morgue somewhere.* The first hijacker's eyes were swollen shut, his nose and mouth a barely recognizable reddish-purple mass. Next to him sat a man whose arm hung limply at an awkward angle; a fine film of sweat covered his gray face. The final man lay facedown on the floor, his ripped pants revealing welts and bruises.

"Lucian and Thad did numbers on all of you. But now it's my turn." She stepped back pointing her finger at each one of them in turn. "Come, you spirits, That tend on mortal thoughts… Make thick my blood."

ॐ

Shreya watched Livia leave, then gazed at the others' confused faces. She slid her hand into Lucian's and looked up. "We need to follow her."

"Too righ'," Thad said, an eyebrow rising as he turned.

Lucian nodded at the Child and followed Thad down to the basement, Annelie close behind.

They found Livia sitting on her heels before the hijacker with the shattered arm, stroking his face. "Wake up," she whispered close to the man's ear. His eyelids twitched. Her lips turned down briefly before her eyes alighted on his arm. A long groan left the man as she ran a finger from his shoulder to his wrist. With a quick motion, she twisted the injured limb.

A pained wail filled the room.

Livia smirked in satisfaction as the man's eyes snapped open. "About time you joined me."

The hijacker snarled, studying her bare shoulders and corset. *"Western whore."* He spat. *"Filth."*

"Is that any way to speak to your hostess?" As her captive tried to pull away, Livia grabbed his uninjured arm, deftly popping the shoulder out of joint. She shifted to the right as vomit spewed from his mouth.

"Ffwrch," Lucian mumbled, wide-eyed. He pulled Shreya back from the bile, not certain if the mess or his lover's behavior surprised him more.

Thad glanced at him. "Fuck is righ'."

Livia gave the hijacker a fang-filled grin and grew quiet as she stared at him, her head cocked to the side.

"Demon cunt." Sweat beaded on his forehead as he tried to push himself away, agony contorting his face.

"Your head really is a muddled mess, Farid. It is okay if I call you by your name, isn't it?" Livia gently took the hand of the man's broken arm and caressed his index finger. "But, I suppose, there are other ways to get you to open up to me." She bent the finger back until she met resistance. "Now, I imagine you're probably just a pissant in the scheme of things, but I'm willing to see what you can tell me anyway. Where and when is the next attack?"

Farid ground his teeth but didn't answer.

"Not talking, huh?" With a flutter of her eyelashes, Livia brought the man's finger down until it touched the back of his hand. She grew quiet again as she played in his mind.

Tears streamed down Farid's face, but his lips pressed together tighter, muffling a building squeal.

Annelie, Thad, and Lucian started at the sudden snap of the hijacker's middle finger.

"Is anyone else gettin' slightly turned on watchin' this?" Thad whispered, glancing at Annelie, who worried at her bottom lip, before meeting Lucian's face.

Lucian glanced at Livia, contemplating the question despite himself, then at Thad, his mouth gaping. "Ew."

Thad shrugged as stifled sobs brought their attention back to Livia.

"Do you feel that, Farid? That ball of ice in your stomach?" Livia asked the man, who nodded reluctantly. "Do you know what it is?" She raised an eyebrow as he shook his head. "No? That's fear. My daughter's fear as she lay bleeding on that plane, feeling her body failing. Fear she'd die so young. Fear she'd never see her parents again. Would you like me to make it stop?"

Farid's head bobbed up and down, his sobs finally escaping.

"Then tell me what I asked for."

"B-B-Belgium. B-Brussels-Midi station. Fourth of December."

Livia patted the man's cheek. "That wasn't so hard, now, was it?" Her mouth curled up. "But, Farid, I lied. I'm not going to make any of this stop." As the hijacker begged, the vampire pushed his ring finger to the back of his hand.

"Enough." Shreya slid her hand from Lucian's grasp and went to Livia, petting her back.

Livia turned her head and studied the girl's face, a dazed look glazing her eyes. "No… I—"

"It *is* enough. He told you what you wanted. Don't journey down that path in front of you. Lucian, please take her upstairs."

Lucian helped Livia to her feet, turning her away from the man as she resisted, and led her from the room quietly.

"What are we going to do with him?" Annelie asked as she and Thad moved closer to the crying hijacker.

Shreya latched onto the man's throat as the two adult vampires watched. A minute later, she let the body slump against the wall and walked toward the stairs; Thad put his hand on her shoulder before she reached them.

"Not so fast, kiddo. Ya can sleep beside Annelie or me tonigh'. Livia may need some time ta… uh… decompress."

Shreya tilted her head, innocent confusion turning the corners of her lips down. A second later, a blush darkened her cheeks. She bobbed her head in understanding.

੭੶੶੶

Livia relaxed as Lucian ran his fingers down her spine, and opened her eyes, studying the smears of blood on the sheets, the walls, and her arm. *Amazing how neat we are when taking a human but how we don't care when we share from one another.*

Without looking, she knew bloody handprints decorated Lucian's chest, back, and buttocks. He'd known she needed to be rough. Every time he moaned his pained pleasure, flinched at the tear of her fangs, or bit into her flesh, her build-up of anger lessened. It finally drained from her completely as he brought her over the crest; she lay on her stomach, trembling.

"I think I know why Bridget was an enforcer… and why she stopped." She turned her head and met his silver eyes as his fingers continued caressing her skin; an eyebrow lifted at her in question. "The feeling... that absolute power we know we have but don't use. You wonder *why* you don't use it once you do. The rush... Nothing like just draining a mugger or rapist. No..." Her teeth grazed her lower lip. "It's a line of cocaine on top of already knowing you're invincible." She reached out and ran a finger down his sweat-and-blood-covered chest.

Lucian nodded slowly, his eyes dark. "I felt that on the plane."

"How easy it must be for people like those hijackers. Knowing they don't face the consequences of their actions... You or I would live an eternity of regret if we didn't care who we killed." Lucian rested his forehead against hers. "Just blow yourself up or crash a plane and never answer for the innocent lives you took with you." A shiver ran through her. "I wasn't happy Shreya stopped me, but now I am. Not caring would be a dangerous addiction for a vampire."

�⧉

The soft glow of lights moved down the clothing racks, shoe racks, and hat cubbies as Livia flicked the switches up. She surveyed the room, deciding on the farthest row, and motioned for the others to follow.

"Doesn' throw anythin' away 'round here, does she?" Thad asked, running his fingers down a perfect reproduction Elizabethan gown.

A corner of Lucian's mouth quirked as he shook his head. He'd seen the theatre's costume "closet" many a time, but it never grew old watching how others reacted to the colorful rows of satin, lace, and velvet.

"I might have to steal one of Livia's costumers to make outfits for my girls." Annelie smiled as she studied a satin corset hanging on another rack.

Thad grunted. "Not sure your strippers need so much, considerin' they'll jus' kick it ta the back a the stage."

Annelie turned, her eyes narrowed, but Thad was halfway to Livia by then. A frustrated breath left her as she met Lucian's face; she abandoned him to join the others at the end of the room.

Lucian shrugged, then slowly made his way through the racks towards them.

"...I'm just sayin', ya two may wanna go more *virginal* looking."

Lucian snorted in amusement as he saw the expressions on Livia's and Annelie's faces.

"The cockies'll be expectin'... I dunno... white. Virgins."

"I'd offer you a spade, but it sounds like you're digging a grave just fine without one." Lucian laughed as the women's faces grew darker.

"C'mon, mate. Look." Thad pointed to the short, black slip Annelie held. "Tell me tha's wha'you'd expect if ya were them."

"Well…" He met Livia's eyes, and then glanced down. "Not really." Livia crossed her arms over her chest. "I'm not saying go for a nun's habit and fawn over them like you've never seen —"

"That's good because it would quickly turn into Castle Anthrax, wouldn't it?"

"You do have a lot of exciting underwear—" Livia punched Lucian's arm as he laughed harder.

Thad rolled his eyes, turning to the nearest clothing rack.

"Castle Anthrax?" Annelie asked, an eyebrow raised.

"Don't tell me you've never seen *Monty Python and the Holy Grail*. Never in two thousand years?" Annelie shook her head as Livia's eyes widened. "Oh, naughty Annelie. I know what we're doing later."

Thad turned back to them, holding up a slinky ivory satin gown. "Now, this—*this*—is more like it." He held it towards Livia with a wide smile. "C'mon. It'd look good on ya!"

Lucian glanced down. Livia mouthed "no" to Thad, but Annelie's eyes lit up like she was a cat staring at a Christmas tree bauble. *Now I see what they had in common,* he thought, shaking his head in amusement.

☜❦☞

The heady aroma of incense roused Badr from his stupor. He inhaled deeply, stretching out on the pillowy couch, and looked down. A silk robe replaced the clothing he'd worn on the plane, and his skin was clean, smelling lightly of musk. "No pain."

His eyes flitted around the huge, dimly lit hall as he pulled himself into a sit. A long table laden with pitchers and bowls full of fruit sat in the center of the room; the aroma of grilled meat wafted to his nostrils, making his stomach growl. The sound of gently lapping water serenaded him from the fountains at either end of the room. He could see others reclining on the couches scattered throughout the hall; their voices filled the hall with a calming susurrus.

"This is… Jannah? Praise be to Allah who has removed from us sorrow." An image of Hadi achieving glory for them flashed through his mind. He looked around, wondering about his partners, before he noticed two *houris* nearing him, their bare feet making soft padding sounds as they walked.

A smile spread across Badr's face as he studied them through his eyelashes. The raven-haired one was clad in a long ivory gown, the darkness of her hair contrasting beautifully with the purity of her clothing. She cradled a pitcher in her delicate hands. The other houri's flowing honey-blond hair spilled over her bare shoulders and fell perfectly over her violet bodice; her skirts swished around her, giving him glimpses of her bare legs. In front of her, she carried a silver tray laden with food.

"Badr," they welcomed in unison, setting their burdens down on the table next to his couch.

They are just as promised: eyes like radiant jewels; chaste gazes; full breasts; young… I wonder how tight they'll be. Immortal, youthful virgins each and every one of them forever. He glanced around the hall, wondering where the rest of his new companions were. *Seventy more…* Blood stirred between his legs as he turned his attention back to the present.

The dark-haired houri poured wine, passing a goblet to the fair one who had eased herself next to Badr. He reached for the second goblet, but she didn't pass it on, instead sitting on his other side and bringing it to her lips. She reached over and plucked a grape from the tray, rolling it slowly between her fingertips.

Badr's mouth watered, thinking of both the fruit and of feeling the woman's fingers on his skin. His lips parted, but the houri reached across him to place the grape in the other's mouth. *Are they teasing me?* He glanced from her to the blonde. "Is this paradise? Jannah?"

The blonde tilted her head, studying him. "Do you believe you were a righteous Muslim? Have you achieved salvation through God's judgement?"

"I do and I have." He squared his shoulders proudly. "I waged jihad on unbelievers as I was told. I've achieved glory for myself and for Allah."

"Ahhh... jihad." The raven-haired one shook her head, her mouth twisting. "How that word has been perverted!"

Badr raised an eyebrow at her.

"I can't help but wonder if you've ever read the Quran." She took a long draught of wine. "It says: *al-jihad fi sabil Allah.* Striving in the path of God."

Badr's jaw went slack.

"I believe you've confused him." The blonde brought her own glass up to her lips.

"I had a feeling I would." A sigh left her. "Badr, jihad is a struggle, and, yes, it's used to mean many types of struggles, war included..." She clapped her hands together, pointing them at him. "But let's go to its purest definition: an *internal* struggle. A struggle against your own evil inclinations... which, I must admit, you lost miserably. Wanting to kill a plane full of people—*unarmed people*—in the name of Islam. Even taken in the military sense, the rules of jihad prohibit you from killing people who aren't engaged in combat."

"B-but they were unbelievers… We must cleanse this world of the unbelievers… Spread Islam… Protect ourselves…" Badr floundered.

"From whom? This isn't the Crusades. No one on that plane was a danger to your religion." The blonde met his gaze, her amethyst eyes catching the dim light like a cat's. "There are many ways to enter Jannah: search for knowledge, build a mosque—"

Badr brought his fist down on his thigh, anger surging through him. "How dare you question my faith? There is to be no quarreling here! You are the houris for my pleasure!"

"Houris?" The raven-haired one laughed. "No."

"We are immortal youths, but houris we are not," the blonde added, an unreadable smile turning the corners of her mouth up. "And you are quite far from Jannah. I doubt any god would ever allow you—or anyone like you—into paradise."

Badr moved to stand, a chill passing through his body, but the women eased him down like he was a child. His head snapped side to side, his hands ready to push them away. "Let me—" He felt his bowels turn to water as the women's bared fangs glistened before meeting his flesh.

Chapter Fifteen

L'Appel Du Vide

May 13, 2014

Bridget slid her finger across a fang, then spread the blood on the puncture wounds on Bastien's neck. He shrugged his shoulder towards the healing skin, scrunching his face in a way she found endearing. The vampire giggled, planting a kiss on his lips. "I know, I know. It itches, but it's better than having people ask about teeth marks on you."

"I could think of stories to tell…" He propped himself up on an elbow, pursing his lips.

"That's what I'm afraid of!" She nipped at him playfully. "Go get some orange juice, and we'll go to Balzar for that lovely beef tartar. You're a bit anemic."

Bastien rose, laughing as his shoulders lifted into an exaggerated shrug. "I wonder why."

Bridget pulled herself into a sit and studied the curve of her lover's backside as he left the room. She slipped her arms into his shirt, inhaling the scent, and relaxed back against the headboard, Bastien's blood spreading warmth throughout her body. Laughter, music, and voices from the Latin Quarter below drifted through the open window in a harmonious serenade; the curtains danced to it as a warm spring breeze floated through.

Bastien's cellphone's chiming pulled her attention from the noises below. Her head moved towards his voice, his words flowing like a melody. *Mmmm… Its sound will never get old…*

As she turned back towards the window, her eyes roaming over the framed photos of his mother, father, brother, and sister, the glint of light on red glass from her lover's nightstand caught her attention. She smiled as she discovered an antique rosary peeking from a silk pouch. Her fingers glided over the faceted beads and filigree crucifix, studying the delicate silver arabesques.

"That was Fèlicien, my broth—" The bottle of juice slipped from his fingers as he noticed the rosary in Bridget's hand. His mouth gaped. "You can touch that?"

"Of course, I—oh…" A corner of Bridget's mouth quirked up. "You thought I couldn't go near holy objects, didn't you?"

Bastien's face reddened as he sat on the bed next to her. *"Peut-être."*

The vampire carefully placed the rosary back in its pouch and snuggled up to her Pet. "It isn't a curse that I have. Holy objects—any belief's—do nothing to affect vampires. In fact, I was torn between erotica and religious objects before I opened the museum. I suppose, some are both anyway." She ran her fingers over his thigh. "Do you still keep your faith?"

"At times, I think, I still believe. Other times, I wonder…" He shook off his thought. "My grand-mère said the Rosary every evening. How I loved watching her!" His arms slid around Bridget, and he eased them down onto the bed, spooning against her. "I've been hiding it when you visit. I was afraid it might burn you."

They shared a quiet laugh, then lay listening to the noises from the street.

"I wonder, sometimes," Bastien started, breaking the stillness, "what God thinks looking at our world. How he could sit by when things turn to *merde*." He hummed deep in his throat. "You've lived through so much of history, seen the best and worst of humanity. Have you never wanted to try to change any of the bad? Never wanted to play god?"

Bridget tilted her head up to glance at him. "I killed Jack the Ripper."

"Really?" His eyes widened as she nodded. "What about now? What would it take?"

"I'm not sure. The Ripper was... maybe partially a whim? There's security in staying out of human affairs... unless it's to be with you." She pressed herself against his chest. "My sire has taken liberties. Annelie enjoyed killing Italian fascists during the Second World War. Being a slave in Rome gave her some lasting biases."

"Rome? *Ancient* Rome?"

"Mmhmm." She raised an eyebrow. "Is your cock getting hard?"

Bastien's cheek warmed against her. "Er... Yes. I've been obsessed with ancient Rome since my teens."

Bridget turned towards him, running her fingers up his leg. "Maybe Balzar can wait then."

"No objections here," he answered, his lips meeting hers.

࿊

Bridget stared up at the moonlit window of the mausoleum, cradling the beads of the rosary to her breast; a stained-glass angel wearing a crown of red roses serenely studied her in return. A heavy sigh left her as she forced herself to turn and meet the words etched into the white marble.

Sébastien Émile Descoteaux
12 juin 1991 —— 13 novembre 2015
Lisieux —— Paris
Non Omnis Moriar

Her fingers traced the letters as tears slid down her cold cheeks.

"You once asked me if I ever wanted to try to change history. What it would take for me to *want* to. I know now." She pressed the palm of her hand to the stone. "This."

Bridget carefully hung the rosary from the handle of the crypt and pulled an envelope from her coat pocket, tying it beside the rosary with a ribbon laced through a corner of it. She brought her lips to the marble. *"Au revoir,* Bastien."

The vampire stroked the stone one last time before joining Natasza in the graveyard.

"The others are expecting us tonight. Are you ready?" the Child asked quietly.

Bridget glanced back at the mausoleum, her heart heavy, then took Natasza's hand.

ॐ

Natasza led Bridget around the back of the Royal Palace of Brussels to a small stone slab hidden behind the shrubbery. The Child pushed the door open, ushering the elder vampire through before sealing it again.

A pleasant rush of warm air enveloped Bridget as she entered the passageway. She straightened slowly, thankful the ceiling was more than tall enough for her to stand upright. "What is this place?" she asked, eyeing the dim fairy lights that hung from the walls, illuminating the way. A tiny smile turned her mouth up. *Quite a knack for decorating.*

"The former palace of Coudenburg. It burnt down in 1731. They built the current palace over it," Natasza answered, taking her hand. "Parts of it are a museum, but we've claimed what the Belgians haven't as ours. They don't have plans to excavate any farther. Makes it the perfect place for us, don't you think?"

"Indeed," Bridget confirmed as they made their way deeper underground, their footsteps the only sounds for a few moments.

"The Children have looked forward to your coming. Ajit's even here. He usually stays close to home—India, that is—but I don't think he would pass on meeting you. You're a legend to us."

"Me? Why? There's nothing special about me."

Natasza stopped short and stared up at her in disbelief. "You truly believe there's nothing special about you? The human child Morning Star helped raise? If you'd encountered her a couple centuries before you did, she would have considered you a sacrifice."

Bridget's stomach flip-flopped; she shifted uncomfortably. "I do know that. It's just…"

"Hard to see her—or Kali—as the criminal that many of the Children still do," the girl finished for her in a whisper. "The Children have good memories and often hold grudges."

She closed her eyes, remembering the warmth of a fire from over a thousand years ago. *Sitting close to the hearth as Annelie teaches me embroidery. Étaín sneaking a look at us as she ties herbs together to dry, a content smile gracing her face.* Her eyelids slowly rose as she looked down at the Child. "Even knowing her past, being shown her actions… She was a mother to me. My protector."

Natasza nodded, a look more knowing than the innocent appearance betrayed in her eyes. "I understand, unfortunately. My adoptive parents were very good to me. And they were also very good Nazis. Nothing is black and white."

Words caught in Bridget's throat as they continued down the passage. *How does Natasza always seem to have the right words?*

❧⚬❦

The passageway opened into a huge room. Some Children lounged on couches, reading or conversing, their youthful voices buzzing with excitement. Others sat watching computer screens at desks lining the back wall, playing games or scrolling through websites.

"This is nothing like I expected," Bridget breathed, her gaze roaming over the top-of-the-line technology the Children were using.

"How else are we going to conquer the world?" Natasza asked.

The elder vampire met the Child's face, wondering at her seriousness. A pleased expression met her; she acknowledged it with a soft laugh. "I believe that's the first joke I've heard you make."

"It looked like you could use a bit of humor." Natasza squeezed Bridget's hand as an awed silence settled around them.

Bridget slowly looked up, her mouth becoming a desert. All the Children's eyes were on her as a boy walked from the back of the room towards them, his strength preceding him as a superheated wave of air. *It's been ages since another vampire sized me up.* She steeled herself and studied him as he approached. *My gods, he wasn't that much younger than I was when he was sired. Twelve to my sixteen, wasn't it? The difference puberty makes to a vampire,* she thought, noticing the vestiges of childhood still on his face. *That little bit of chubbiness modern teens hate to think about.* She scanned his hoodie, Converse high-tops, and loose jeans as he neared. *How did I think he'd dress?*

Ajit pushed a lock of dark hair under his knit cap as he stopped, his amber eyes level with hers. He eased the push of his strength, and his face softened, though an underlying look of teenage boredom remained. Without a word, he wove his arm into hers and led her from the room, Natasza following.

৵৽৵

Ajit led them down the stone passageway to a smaller chamber and motioned for Bridget to sit in an armchair. He took another, lounging back with a leg over the arm, as Natasza made herself comfortable on a nearby sofa.

Bridget avoided the Original's eyes though she could feel them on her, instead looking at the TV monitors behind him. Images from the streets of Brussels flashed before her. *What would all those people think if they knew who was watching them?* She bit her tongue, holding back the nervous giggle threatening to leave her at the thought of humans trying to interact with the Children.

"You seem uncomfortable. You've met my cousin. You've met my aunt." A discernible note of disgust tinged Ajit's voice at the mention of Kali. "Why? What's different about me?"

Bridget let her eyes roam over the CCTV monitors another minute before meeting his expectant gaze. "I get the feeling you aren't quite as happy to be meeting me as they were."

"It may have been the approach," Natasza mumbled, rolling her eyes.

"You know what the Children expect of me, Natasza." Ajit glanced at her then back to Bridget. "Your reputation precedes you. Morning Star's special one, Kali's enforcer. I had to see for myself how strong you really are. You didn't disappoint."

"How nice to learn," Bridget replied dryly, suppressing a sudden twinge of annoyance she felt building inside of her.

"Contrary to what you believe, I am quite excited to be meeting you." He swung his leg off the arm of the chair to face her more directly. "You're one of the few vampires who can claim precognition. I've encountered some humans and Children who have it, but neither are long for the world."

Bridget shifted and shook her head, anger at herself growing in her chest. "It does me little good."

"Because you choose to ignore it. Because you're strong enough to keep the visions at bay." He paused. "You regret that now."

"Yes." She fought back burning tears at the image of Bastien's lifeless eyes staring up at her. *His death could have been avoided... maybe all those deaths could have been.*

"You let small things in. Feelings. Completely open yourself again. It's been centuries. Let me see."

Bridget saw the worried look on Natasza's face before Ajit's gaze caught hers. Her eyelids closed as she focused inward. Nausea rolled through her as the wall inside her mind slipped down. Clutching her temples, she bowed her head, her brain burning with the flood of events flowing through it. Times and places of important births, deaths, wars, and treaties poured from her lips. A tremor brought her to her knees in front of the chair. *Did it hurt this much before?* She slammed the wall in her mind back up.

Tears washed down her face. "Why would you want to see that? Why make me do that?" she asked, wiping blood from her nose and looking up at Ajit.

Natasza wrapped her arms around Bridget as Ajit slid from his chair and knelt in front of her.

"Because you had to do it," he replied, his voice cracking slightly. "You needed to remember how powerful you are. And you need to use that if you're going to make a difference."

‽∾

Bridget surveyed the Brussels-Midi train station. Crowds of people moved to and from platforms; some eagerly catching trains to take them on weekend escapes while others were happily returning from a day at work. A cacophony of voices surrounded her. She glanced over at the nearby foodcourt, noticing a couple drinking and laughing over glasses of beer.

"What should we toast to tonight?" Bastien poured them each a glass of wine, then leaned in.

"Hmmm…" Her eyes roamed over the playful look on his face. *"The beautiful weather."* He laughed as she pulled out her phone. *"Smile for me before we drink."*

He swirled the wine in his glass and held it up to her, giving her a mischievous half smile.

"Parfait." With a tap, she captured the moment. She picked up her glass and clinked it against his. *"To this beautiful November evening… and you."*

"Five-fifteen. They'll be coming through soon," Natasza announced, squeezing her hand.

Bridget nodded down at the Child. She thought of the other Children, waiting scattered throughout the station, ready to defuse bombs and sabotage guns. Her stomach danced with nervous excitement. *Almost time.*

Her gaze wandered back over to the couple in the foodcourt just as the woman raised her phone to take a picture of the man. *That won't be the last photo you ever get together,* the vampire mused. *I promise you that.*

Chapter Sixteen

Aftershocks

November 26, 2015

"This is not the way I wanted to spend Thanksgiving," FBI Agent Sinead Moss groaned, knowing she was disappointing her daughter and husband by working yet another holiday. The long hours had been taking a toll on her marriage. This wouldn't help the situation.

She rewinded her videos for the fifth time. "How the *hell* did I lose two hours' worth of interviews? They were the first two off the friggin' plane! I know they were interviewed—I interviewed Llewellyn and Mike did Boyd!" She gulped down the remnants of her coffee, grimacing at the lukewarm temperature. "Ugh. Like that helps this crappy coffee."

Agent Moss sat back in her chair and spun herself back and forth in a half-circle, trying to recall what Lucian Llewellyn had told her during questioning. Her mind hit a wall, but the rhythm of her movement lulled her into a trance as she remembered his calm voice.

"Sinead?"

She started, knocking her mug to the carpet. "Dammit…"

"Sorry about that. Least it was empty." Agent Mike Ashe picked the mug up, rolling it in his palms.

Agent Moss eyed him, knowing her partner's nervous tic never brought good news. "What's up, Mike?" She put her hands over his to stop the movement.

"Well—" he set the mug on her desk "—our hijackers seem to have, um, disappeared."

Her brow drew down, her brain not registering his words. "Disappeared? How do three badly wounded men disappear? They didn't just wander off! They could barely walk when we took them from the plane. They were on their way to the hospital."

"They never made it. Agent B.P. Thaddeus was the last who signed for them… and no one seems to know where he took them or who the hell he is, for that matter."

Agent Moss covered her face with her hands. "Jesus Christ on a goddamn cracker… We are so fu—" The buzz of her phone cut her off. "Crap. It's Madison." She steeled herself for her superior's wrath. "Hello, sir…"

Agent Ashe watched as relief passed over his partner's face, his own nerves unknotting at her smile.

"Yes, sir. Happy Thanksgiving to you as well!" She hung up the phone, looking up. "According to Madison, the prisoners were delivered to USP Lee early this morning. He told us to go home and enjoy the holiday."

His shoulders lifted briefly. "Sounds good to me. Happy Thanksgiving, Sinead! Don't eat too much."

"Same to you! See you Monday." Sinead Moss stood, pulling on her coat and shoving her laptop in her briefcase as she thought about the smile that would be on her child's face. She pushed down the light switch as she left, glancing back with a shake of her head. "Now let's hope I find those two missing interviews."

కాలో

November 28, 2015

Heidi Pasternak pushed turkey and mashed potatoes around her plate, her mind thousands of miles away. She looked up, the feel of Bryan's gaze finally pulling her back to the present. "Sorry, babe. Were you saying something?"

"No," her husband answered with a soft chuckle. "Just wondering how you were doing though. Thanksgiving was a bit intense, what with the barrage of questions. Kinda hoped Christmas shopping'd take your mind off things for a little while."

"It did." She forced a smile. "Happy to have it all out of the way!"

"Then why the faraway look?"

Heidi set her fork down and laced her fingers together, leaning her elbows on the table. "I've been trying really hard to *forget*… to accept the… um… incident as what it was: luck or fate or whatever. But stuff doesn't add up! It's driving me nuts!"

Bryan cocked his head. "What'd'ya mean? What stuff?"

"I don't know… everything. The guns, the guys who stopped the hijacking. The—that girl." Shaking her head, she relaxed back in her chair. "I know you told me not to look, but when have I ever listened?" She laughed nervously as he mouthed "never." "Exactly. Well, I know that girl was dying. Her skin was sheet white. Then… that guy, I don't know, but I think he kissed her…"

"Like, mouth-to-mouth?"

"Come on. We both know that wouldn't have stopped someone from bleeding to death."

"True…" Bryan furrowed his brow. "But a kiss?"

"I swear to you, *that's* what I saw. He kissed her, and she woke up a minute later."

Bryan took another bite of his food, chewing slowly as he mulled over his wife's words.

"Maybe… nah, never mind. You'll think I'm crazy."

"Go 'head and tell me. I already know you're crazy."

"Jerk." She threw her napkin at him, grinning. "I think —and you know full well I'm not religious—I think those two were angels. They knew those guns were fake. They rained holy hell down on the hijackers. The bombs that one had didn't go off. And that girl lived when she shouldn't have."

Bryan took her hands in his and kissed her knuckles. "There's a lot in this world that we don't know about. Angels? Maybe. More likely, they saw they had nothing to lose. Like that plane full of people who fought back on nine-eleven."

Heidi blinked back tears. "But all those people died."

"Yeah," he answered, swallowing down the reminder hard. "But they fought. I don't know what stroke of luck—or divine intervention—we had on that flight, but we had something protecting us that night." He stood, pulling his wife to her feet. "And, as much as I want to dwell on it, what I want more is to appreciate the chance it gives us. Come to bed, Mrs. Pasternak."

She laughed. "It's only seven."

Bryan waggled his eyebrows. "I said come to bed, not go to sleep. We have to get started on the children we're going to tell the tale of Mommy and Daddy's return flight from their honeymoon…"

December 5, 2015

Cassie Lynn set the book she'd been reading down on her nightstand, clicked off the light, and rolled over, pulling the blankets around her and drifting off.

Was it the sobs and screams or the heat of the bonfire that woke her? She wasn't certain, but she was certain she wasn't viewing the world through her own eyes when she opened them.

The stench assaulted her nose, seeping into her taste buds, as she came to. The rank bouquet of sweat, urine, and shit made her head ache worse.

Chains clanked as she moved her arms. No, not her *arms. The forearms were muscular, strong. A man's arms. She flexed the fingers, feeling the stiffness.*

"Stay still, ya ass! He'll see ya move!" the woman to her right hissed. Tears carved clean lines down her filthy face.

"Do ya think tha' matters?" a voice snapped. Cassie Lynn turned her head to the left. A man broad in the shoulders smirked at her. The name Owen flashed through her head. "He's comin' for alla us. Been at it for a time now. Look." He nodded to the right. "He'll be here soon."

Cold fear washed down her spine, her heart hammering, her breath coming in painful gasps. Warm wetness spread through the front of her pants.

As she watched, the shadowy figure straddled the woman to her right, the woman's scream getting lost in those of the others. The shadow's head arched back, and then it struck like a snake. A minute later, it ripped open its wrist, flooding the woman's mouth with its blood. The woman's screams began anew as she writhed in agony.

The shadow was on Cassie Lynn next, its onyx eyes studying her curiously. She stared back, every inch of her wanting to turn away from the dusky face but unable to. You're mine now, *growled through her mind as teeth like needles pierced her neck.*

Cassie Lynn snapped awake, her hair sticking to the cold sweat on her cheeks. "What the fuck was that?" She pushed herself into a sit and pulled open her nightstand drawer, retrieving her journal. A shiver passed through her as she flipped through the pages, stopping to skim recent entries, events and emotions she had experienced vividly: the glorious freedom of riding horseback behind a herd of cattle; pride swelling her chest at an auburn-haired woman presenting a child; joy while playing with a boy who she somehow knew resembled the man whose memories she was dreaming. Other odd snippets of times and places, but nothing as terrifying as what she'd just dreamt. She grabbed her pen and started writing down all the details.

❧

December 11, 2015

Renè Descoteaux inhaled a deep breath before entering his family's mausoleum, but it didn't ease the heaviness in his chest. It never did. He tried to smile the way Bastien always had at the colors from the stained-glass window playing on the white marble.

"Bastien, this is a solemn place. You must stop grinning and be serious," Delphine chided.

"But, Maman, it is too beautiful to be sad here."

His stomach twisted, but he forced himself to where his son lay interred.

"Hello, Bastien. It hurt not coming last week. Couldn't think of something to tell your mother to get out of the house. At least Maman doesn't know how much I come. She'd realize I... No matter." He shook his head and stood silent for a minute, mindlessly studying the silvery swirls in the marble, before pressing his palm to his son's name.

Renè swallowed the lump that had grown in his throat before focusing on the etching. *Twenty-four. At twenty-four, I was holding you in my arms for the first time, mon dauphin.* Blood pounded through his ears as thoughts of the recent failed terrorist attacks flooded his brain. "Why couldn't the one that killed you have been like that?" He rested his forehead on the cold stone, and his hand balled into a fist. "Mon fils..." The tears he wouldn't —*couldn't*— let his wife and younger children see streamed down his face. "This world makes no sense to me now... I can't..."

His heart skipped a beat as he realized he'd made his decision. He squeezed his eyes shut. *Dear God, forgive me. Help my love Delphine and Fèlicien and Alix to forgive me. They don't know how I died with Sèbastien.*

As his eyes opened, a stray sunbeam reflecting off silver and red glass caught his attention. His mother's rosary swayed gently from the crypt handle, an envelope tied beside it with a green ribbon. "We looked all over for these." He scooped up the beads, wondering who could have brought them, then untied the envelope, carefully unsealing it.

Two photographs accompanied by a letter met him. In the first photo, Bastien held up a glass of wine to the photographer, a half smile decorating his face. The next photo showed his son dancing with a redheaded woman, her long hair hiding her features, in front of a moonlit Eiffel Tower. Warmth spread through Renè despite the chill permeating the stone building.

He unfolded the letter, surprised to see it addressed to him, and read the beautifully flowing script:

Dearest Renè,

Though we've never met, I feel like I know you well from Bastien's stories. He spoke so fondly of his family that I feel I know all of you! But you need this letter more than they do, and I know you'll find it along with the rosary.

I feel how broken you are. You're dying every moment you think of your son. You imagine his fear and his pain, his last moments.

Can I tell you Bastien felt no pain or fear when he died? I honestly cannot. One moment he was holding me as I lay injured. The next he was gone. So quickly that I couldn't do anything but register the sudden helplessness—and emptiness.

But your emptiness and grief is consuming you. You're thinking of taking your own life. Bastien was your firstborn, your prince, and he wouldn't have wanted you to abandon his mother, brother, and sister. He'd want you to live, cherish his memory, smile like he was wont to do when he visited the mausoleum, feel warmth thinking of his life—a warmth like those photos gave you. Feel something other than sorrow.

You need to live for Bastien. Let your wife know you need her because she needs you, too. Be there for your son and daughter. And, even though you don't know me, live for me because I loved your son.

Toujours,

B

Renè glanced around him, hoping whomever had written the letter was nearby. He eased himself to the cold stone floor and placed the photos beside him. His head rested back against the wall as his fingers caressed the crucifix; he closed his eyes, remembering the order of the prayers, and crossed himself slowly. "O Lord, open my lips;

O God, come to my aid; O Lord, make haste to help me…"

January 2, 2016

"… and now we have the latest footage of the failed New Year's Day attack at Madrid-Barajas Airport. Security cameras and eye-witness video show bystanders tackling the suspects when they realize their bombs and guns have failed…"

"Mistress."

Nunzia ignored her Pet's whisper and continued tapping her fingernail on the diner table in boredom. *Why do we stay in this horrid country?* She glanced down at her Pet's plate of half-eaten pork roll and eggs. *An affront to the food gods.*

"Mistress."

The vampire took a sip of coffee. *They can't even get that right. Nona, forgive me. I'll have to find a Starbucks.*

"Mistress!"

Nunzia glanced up, noticing waitresses and other customers turning in their direction. She shot a woman at the counter a half-innocent, half-warning look, and turned to Wil with fire in her eyes. *"What?"*

Wil cowered at her gaze while motioning up to the TV. He lowered his voice. "Mistress, who are they? Can everyone see what they are?"

Though the footage was shaky and people ran in front of the person holding the camera, Nunzia could make out two vampires standing back from the madness, a petite redhead holding the hand of a blonde child. *Bridget? Well, there's a bad penny... And a child? Who the hell sired a child?* She gently took his chin in her thumb and forefinger, letting her gaze soften to ease his mind. "No, Pet, not everyone. You know you're special." Her eyes went back up to the screen. *Pepi is going to want to see this.*

Part Three

"Every person must choose how much truth he can stand."
Irvin D. Yalom

Chapter Seventeen

Shock and Awe

Livia, Lucian, Thad, and Annelie looked up as Shreya entered the living room. The Original had long since abandoned her sari and bindi, instead opting for something she called more "modern": a pair of denim overalls over a brightly colored t-shirt and a tiny pair of Chuck Taylors. "I've had news from Natasza." She hopped up on the couch beside Livia. "There's a terrorist cell operating not far from us. Alexandria, Virginia. They're planning a series of attacks in the Washington, D.C., area."

"Bridget heard that from… Belgium?" Lucian tilted his head to the side, his eyes widening.

Annelie laughed. "It shouldn't be surprising. I told you she was *very* good at being Kali's enforcer."

The Original shook her head, her mahogany ponytail swinging side to side. "Bridget didn't just listen this time. She opened herself back up."

Annelie's expression of pride vanished, replaced by one of concern.

"Opened herself back up? What's tha' mean?" Thad glanced at the others, avoiding Annelie, then back to Shreya.

"Letting her precognitive abilities free," Shreya answered, her cheeks dimpling as she smiled softly.

"Anythin' that little redhead can' do?" Wonder spread over Thad's face.

"She's let stuff in for a long time, hasn't she?" Livia asked, bringing her legs onto the couch and tucking them under her.

"Not like she *can*," Annelie breathed. "She can... she sees so much. She had the ability when she was a human but not to the same extent. When I sired her..." Her mouth moved, searching for the right words. "It took months for her to learn to control it. The flood of information. It's painful, leaves her exhausted." She worried at her bottom lip, her teeth grazing the metal hoop through it. "And that was long ago. The things that must be coming to her now, with so many more people on Earth."

Shreya studied the vampires around her, their concern hanging heavy in the air. "I think you all underestimate her, though you should know better by now."

"We don't underestimate her," Livia said, shaking her head. "We've seen what she's capable of. Are in awe of it.

But, as invincible as she is—as we all are—we worry because we love her."

Shreya met her eyes, confused.

Annelie leaned in. "Do you never feel that way about Ajit or Natasza or any of the other Children?"

"Perhaps." A corner of Shreya's lips pursed as she thought. "But there's a large part of me that says worry about them is a waste of my energy. All the Children are strong, and they take care of themselves." The Original reached out, touching Annelie's hand. "My worry goes to humans—child and adult alike—more. There's only an illusion of control that they have."

"Some a us know that better than others." Thad's gaze shifted briefly to Annelie, and a shadow darkened his eyes as he looked back at Shreya. "It's not a lesson ya forget."

"But you forget I know that firsthand... though, what did I truly know at four years old?" Shreya whispered, sadness lacing her voice.

Thad stared down at his lap, running the knuckle of his index finger down the bridge of his nose. "I did forget... I apologize."

"What matters is we have control now." Shreya's sadness disappeared as her eyes, alight with purpose, roamed over the adults' faces. "No matter how we came into this. And we have work to do."

❧

Sinead Moss and Mike Ashe glanced at one another as Special Agent Madison clicked to a slide of an office building. Another briefing, another late night in the works. "… The financial activity we've been observing has finally led us to a cell of six potential terrorists in the Alexandria, Virginia, vicinity. We haven't been able to determine what exactly they're planning, but with their proximity to D.C., it can't be anything good. They meet once a week in the offices of one of the members of the cell. We have all the warrants we need. Be at the ready the night after tomorrow."

"Back at the grind," Mike grumbled, rising to his feet and gathering his pen and binder.

"Yeah. At least it's close to home… as horrible as that sounds to say." Sinead pouted, thinking about how her absence had been affecting her husband and daughter. *Ted knew I'd have to be away. He can't take this out on me.* She shook her head as she gathered her things. The thought didn't remove her guilt. She wished it would.

࿇

"Don't say it." Lucian's eyes narrowed as he watched the others' reactions to his appearance.

Livia held back the grin playing on her mouth. "I wasn't going to say a thing."

Annelie pressed her lips together and made a zipping motion across them.

"I was." Thad laughed as his eyes roamed up the other vampire's suit, shoes, and tie, then came to rest on Lucian's head.

Lucian self-consciously ran a hand over his hair, cut short and "business-like" according to Livia. He shifted from one foot to the other, uncomfortable after not having worn anything but jeans and t-shirts for years. The cheap fabric of the off-the-rack suit made him long for his tailor's expertise.

"Nah, mate. Ya look good. Better than havin' a man bun."

"I'd rather have the man bun," Lucian mumbled, frowning.

Livia reached up and brushed her fingers over Lucian's temple. "It's only a night. They're expecting business people. When you wake up tomorrow evening, it will all be back. And you know it."

"Ehhh... I know. It just feels so... *naked*." He studied himself in the mirror behind Livia, teasing the shorn ash-blond locks.

"Naked is never a bad look either." Thad waggled his eyebrows.

Lucian shook his head, a corner of his mouth quirking. "Not happening."

"With just me or...?" Thad gave him a coy smile, running his hands down the lapels of the suit he wore.

"The thought of another man's hairy arse does absolutely nothing for me."

"For the record, ma ass is far from hairy. And ya've gotta be the only truly straigh' vampire I know, mate!"

"I really didn't need to know that about your arse." Lucian met Thad's amazed face with a look of doubt. "The only one? Really?" He glanced at Annelie and Livia, who shrugged their shoulders and looked away, realizing Thad was right. "Christ… I really am the only one…"

"The only what?" Shreya asked, joining them.

Lucian floundered, feeling uncomfortable, despite the Original's likely knowledge, discussing sexuality with her.

"Straigh' vampire."

"Thad!" Livia raised an eyebrow at him.

Shreya broke down in giggles. "It's okay, Livia. I've been around five thousand years. I know what sexuality and sex are." She glanced around the adult vampires. "We Children may not partake, but we're quite observant about the goings-on of adults. And, I must say, there is *a lot* to observe. The Children, like human children, are curious about the ways of the world." An ornery look spread over her face as Livia, Lucian, Thad, and Annelie shifted uncomfortably. She shook her head. "Don't think about it. We'd better get going."

"We?" Annelie studied her. "You're joining in on this?"

"I can't let you guys have all the fun all of the time." Shreya skipped from the room.

⇜⇝

"How's this goin' ta go?" Thad asked as the five vampires stopped at the entrance to the office building. The others looked at one another.

Livia bit her lip. "I guess we hadn't really thought of it. They're expecting us. I mean, they think they're meeting with investors to fund a 'project.' "

"No shock an' awe then?" Thad pouted. "There goes the fun."

"What did you think the suits were for?" Annelie shook her head as Thad shrugged. "I set up meetings with them, making them believe we were sympathetic to their cause."

A dainty grunt left Shreya. "I appreciate your work, Morning Star, but these people don't deserve to feel safe at all. They were planning to attack public parks—along with government buildings—during the busiest hours. We go with shock and awe." Light from a nearby streetlight glinted in her smoky eyes. "They wanted to kill as many innocents as possible. I'm going in first. Follow me. Make them feel the terror they would have inflicted on others… then we'll have a convenient gas leak to dispose of the evidence." The Original opened the door, her spine straightening as she walked down the hallway. "Come on!"

"So I cut my hair for nothing?" Lucian grumbled as they followed the Original into the building.

৵৽

Sinead Moss and Mike Ashe watched Madison's hand gestures and listened to his hushed instructions through their earpieces, moving in closer to the small office building. The modern brick buildings surrounding the group of federal agents stared down with dark, empty windows. They had closed off the street earlier in the day, feigning work on a water main, but the sounds of cars drifted to them from a block away.

Thank God no one is around. Sinead studied the abandoned street, thinking about how close to innocent people radical terrorists operated. *Then again, the men and women who commit these crimes were once innocent people, weren't they?*

Mike turned to her, his nose wrinkling in disgust. "You smell that?" he whispered, pushing a finger to his ear to ask the team.

"Shit! That's gas!" replied another agent.

Sinead lifted her chin, inhaling deeply and catching the odor. She froze, her pulse racing, as five shadowy figures moving between buildings distracted her from the present. *Who the hell are they? That man…he looks like—*

Mike tapped her shoulder, bringing her attention back. She looked back to where she'd seen the figures. *No one there.*

"All right, everyone, back up."

Sinead followed her team in its retreat, shaking off the feeling of seeing people who couldn't possibly be there. She glanced back from their alley hiding place, thankful to be clear of the rank smell of gas.

"We need to call—" Madison's words were cut off as the shockwave of an explosion rocked the agents, knocking them against one another and the buildings surrounding them.

"Is everyone all right?" Madison's breathless voice came through her ear.

Sinead looked at her teammates, disbelief and relief mingling on the faces of everyone around her. But, miraculously, no one appeared injured other than ringing ears.

"That was a close one," Mike groaned, letting his head ease back onto the brick wall.

"Guess we weren't meant to get those guys. Fitting end, though, wouldn't you say?"

Agent Moss laughed, forgetting about the figures she thought she had seen, and wiped a hand down her cheek. "You could say that, Mike, you could say that. Too bad it doesn't save us from any paperwork."

☜⋆☞

*Alexandria, Virginia—Six bodies have been
recovered from the rubble of the Zeigler Building
after an explosion occurred Tuesday at 8:30 pm.*

Authorities are working on identifying the victims as well as investigating the cause of the explosion.

Chapter Eighteen

Waking Up

January 31, 2014

Bridget paused as she approached the Musée National du Moyen-Age to watch Bastien as he waited for her. He sat on a low wall, his thumbs typing away on his mobile phone, as the sun descended, the collar of his peacoat up to shield his face from the winter air. A breeze tousled his hair. A corner of his mouth lifted when he saw her, and he rose to his feet, leaning down to kiss her gently on the cheek when she reached him.

"Bonsoir. Ça va?"

"Très bien maintentant," she replied, her skin tingling from the touch of his warm lips. "Aren't you freezing? Didn't you finish work a half an hour ago?"

Bastien lifted his messenger bag onto his shoulder and turned down his collar. "I haven't been out here long. My sister texted. I think she knows I'm keeping something from her." His head tilted down towards her in indication. "I like to keep special people to myself at first… and you seem like a private person."

Bridget's hand slid into his as they started down the sidewalk. "I've learned it's easier to stay away from issues that way." He nodded. "How old is your sister?"

"Sixteen. Alix is the youngest of us. I don't think my parents were prepared for a teenage girl after two boys." A soft laugh left him. "Plus, she's hard of hearing, so if she doesn't want to listen… you get the idea."

"Is anyone ever ready for a sixteen-year-old girl, hard of hearing or not?" she returned playfully. *How different that age must be now. I was married, on the verge of motherhood when I was a human at sixteen.*

They walked in silence for a block before Bastien spoke. "I was thinking… I don't have class on Tuesdays and the museum isn't open…" He motioned back towards the direction they left. "Maybe we could spend the day together. Musée d'Orsay? Lunch there if we beat the crowds?"

"I…" Bridget inclined her head up to meet his expectant gaze. "Can't." A quiet breath left her as his face fell and she felt his body stiffen slightly.

The corners of his mouth turned up halfheartedly; his eyes returned to the sidewalk in front of them. "I'm starting to think you don't want to be seen with me in the daylight."

Her stomach churned as she felt his frustration build. *I want nothing more than to be with you every minute of the day and night.* She inhaled. "I think there are some things I should tell you…"

ॐ∼ॐ

"When did he learn what you are? How?" Ajit's voice broke Bridget's reverie.

She met his face, an eyebrow lifted in amusement, as he sat down in the chair catty-corner from her.

"I wasn't poking around in your head, I promise. It's never something I do casually." He slung a leg over the arm of the chair as he reclined back. "You get this look in your eyes. It's sad but somehow *not* at the same time. Reminiscent is the word maybe?"

Bridget swallowed down the lump in her throat. "That's probably the right word." A long breath passed her lips. "How does anyone ever find out what we are? It's either in their last moments alive or we show them because we want them to be ours as a Pet or a fledgling." She opened her memories to him.

Bastien stopped walking, the words registering in his mind. "Merde. You're married. Or… you're as young as you look."

Bridget ran her thumb over his wrist, feeling his pulse quicken as he weighed the possibilities. "No, it's a little more complicated than either of those." He eyed her, worry spreading over his features. "And I'm not dying." His eyebrows drew down; she felt the confusion go through him as he wondered how she knew what he was thinking. "Let's go to your flat. I don't want to tell you in the middle of Boulevard Saint Germain."

They walked the remaining two blocks and three flights of stairs to his apartment, silent as the people in the street around them chattered. Bridget let the mask she'd had blocking him from noticing her preternatural eyes and skin slip as he hung up their coats.

Bastien wobbled, then steadied himself against the wall. "I must need to eat," *he said, bringing a hand to his head as he turned back around. His eyes widened, and he took a step back, blinking hard.* "Merde… Are you sure you're not dying? Your skin…"

Bridget patted the cushion next to her; he sat down, reaching out his hand to touch her cheek. "Not dying." *She met his eyes and held his fingers to her face, enjoying the warmth of his skin.* "Never dying. I'm immortal. A vampire."

He inhaled sharply. "Merde."

Ajit slid from her memory. "He took it better than some."

"He did." She held back a grin, remembering Bastien's curious, excited barrage of questions. *"Chérie, you can't hold back on a history major after telling him you've lived thousands of years!"*

The Original studied her, eyes narrowing as he thought. "Do you ever wonder how the rest of the world would react if they found out about us? Part of me wonders if it will happen now with what we're doing. The fear, the hatred they'd have. They can't even accept one another being different races or religions. A different species entirely would mentally fuck them." His eyes grew dark for a moment. "Then again, some morbid part of me longs for the human race to know about us."

Bridget shivered at Ajit's statement. *Chaos. They'd never all accept us... and it wouldn't go over well for them.* "What happens if they do learn about us en masse?"

"I'm sure my aunt would love to have you back full force in your old job," he answered, disgust creeping into his words.

Her gaze fixed on him as a heavy silence blanketed the room. "Will you ever forgive her for the things she's done?"

Ajit's lips parted but closed again before any sound came out; he met her face. "When Shreya and I killed that child in Banawali—sealed our family's fate—we didn't know any better. We were *true* children then, and the hunger clouded what little judgment we had. Nothing like what we are and have after five thousand years on this earth." He drummed his thumb on the arm of his chair. "Our aunt, though... I don't care how angry she was. She had children of her own, suffered the pain of losing them when we were attacked. We thought she was better than she was. And I don't think I could forgive her for that disappointment." A shoulder lifted indifferently. "Then again, it's been millennia. Maybe one day Shreya will convince me it's not worth holding on to."

An image of the diminutive Original's young face floated through Bridget's mind, turning the corners of her mouth up. "Shreya seems like she could be *quite* persuasive if she wants to be."

"You have no idea!" The first true smile Bridget had seen from Ajit spread across his face, but it faded quickly. "Where do we need to go next?"

She closed her eyes and let the wall in her mind slowly descend, filtering the information that flowed to her. "Egypt and… Las Vegas. On the same day." A chill ran through her.

"It's a good thing Morning Star calls Las Vegas home then. I'd offer to send Children to help out, but I doubt any would volunteer."

"Probably not." Bridget sighed. *And you'll never let my sire live down her past either, Ajit.*

"Egypt, hm?" He lifted an eyebrow. "Your abilities seem to want to get us closer to the center of the problem."

"Maybe we could end those responsible once and for all," she replied, an odd feeling of calm washing over her at the thought.

⤙⤚

The television droned on in the next room, making Cassie Lynn's eyelids heavy.

"Got her good a few times... She's fadin'..." The man whose memories she was reliving swallowed painfully, forcing saliva down his throat.

This is the first time the man's spoken in these dreams. I know that voice...

"Help her. I'll take care of that one."

She watched through his eyes as the speaker strode down the aisle. Lucian? That's the plane we were on. *The man's dread overcame her confusion as something thudded against his chest.*

"No, no, no..." His hand cradled a clammy cheek, turning the face up. "Look at me. Wake up!" Her own eyes opened in front of her.

This isn't real. This is a dream. Please wake up for real, Cassie Lynn!

"Thad?" Yes! That's it—Thad's voice! *"I'm so cold." Cassie Lynn watched herself struggle for air as a violent tremor shook her body.*

A ball of fear slammed Thad, and Cassie Lynn somehow knew it was her own fear, not his. "Nah, you're fine, I promise. Justa scratch." The slowing beats of her heart thudded in Thad's ears as he scanned the faces of the other passengers. How the hell am I gonna do this with everyone watchin'? *flowed through both of their minds.*

"No, it's not. My arm's off." A soft sigh followed the statement.

Shit, shit, shit. *Pain, blood, and the smoky taste of whiskey flooded Thad's mouth as he brought his lips down to hers, slipping his injured tongue through them.*

Cassie Lynn woke and ran to the bathroom, her dinner splashing into the toilet bowl. She rose to brush her teeth and then rinsed her face, trying to shake the image of herself dying in Thad's arms from her mind. "What the hell happened to me?"

Chapter Nineteen

What Happens in Vegas

Carson City—Federal agents raided a Reno apartment Tuesday night, arresting six men in connection with a suspected terror plot. Authorities recovered two vans loaded with materials to make explosives. The suspects had been discussing their plans with an undercover FBI agent via a social media website for two weeks. The correspondence indicated that the suspects planned to drive the vans onto the Las Vegas Strip, hitting as many people as they could before detonating the explosives…

Agent Sinead Moss stared down at the article, the images from the night still fresh in her mind. After fifteen years in the bureau and more than a few raids in that time —none of which were run-of-the-mill—she still thought there was something more off than usual about these suspects.

What was that one screaming about as we handcuffed him? Get the voice out of his head? Crazier than most I've encountered… and that's saying a lot! And how relieved they looked when we put them in the cars…

Her eyes migrated to the photographs above the article. "Who's he? I thought I knew all the agents there that evening." She brought the newspaper closer to her face, squinting at a man in one shot.

"Looks like that guy from the plane. Thad Boyd," Sinead muttered to herself, her head cocking to one side. She shook her head with a laugh. "Yeah, okay, Sinead. First, you think you see him in Alexandria. Now here. You really need some sleep!" She tossed the paper on the kitchen table and pushed her chair away, stretching as she stood.

She slipped into bed and wrapped her arm around her husband's waist, but he moved it off gently. *Can't win them all.* She slid from bed, grabbed her pillow, and headed for the spare bedroom for the tenth night in a row, checking in on Lydia as she went.

৵৽৻

Thad started as Annelie tossed the newspaper onto his chest. She stood in front of him, arms crossed over her breasts, as he reclined on the sofa in Kali's Cabaret's office. "You're in one of the photos."

He grabbed the paper, examining the part she had folded to the beat of the music below. "Well, fuck me dead. There I am." His shoulders lifted. "Least I shaved for it."

"Seriously? That's *all* you can say?" Her eyes roamed over his face as she shook her head. "Do you know how much danger that puts us in? One of those agents could've recognized you from before! Idiot."

Thad sat up, putting the paper on the table beside him, and released a slow breath. Annelie made it clear every day that she didn't like how he did things, not that he had wanted to be there. The thought of his former lover feeding from children still turned his stomach. *Kali was at least honest with me about herself when she hired me.* But, since none of the Children of the Night volunteered to help with the upcoming intervention, Shreya had convinced him to join Annelie in Las Vegas. *Couldn' say no ta an Original, could ya, Thaddy? Not like ya ever say no ta Kali, either.*

"Lemme get this straigh'. Ya think that—" he pointed to the paper "—is gonna expose vampires ta the world? Not, say, Lucian's face on the back a his books, Livia an' her *well-known* theatre company—"

"Just… stop. Listen, I know you didn't want to be here and I didn't want…" Annelie stiffened as she looked up at the doorway behind Thad.

Thad followed her eyes and rose to his feet beside her, a wave of abhorrence rolling over him from Annelie's direction. *Only one immortal can cause that reaction.*

He studied the vampire before him, Annelie's estranged sire. The Ancient stood quietly just inside the doorway, his perfectly tailored pinstripe suit giving him the air of a business executive. Jet lashes framed his amber eyes; the soft light of the room cast a warm glow on his smooth, shaved head. An aura of dangerous power and sensuality radiated around him. *Fancies himself somethin'. Then again, wasn' he a pharaoh?*

"Hello, Annelie." The vampire's gaze slid over her schoolgirl outfit, then met her face, his lips rising into a cocksure smile. "It's been a long time."

"Centuries. I liked it that way, Pepi," she replied, covering her bare midriff with her arms. "Why are you here?"

Pepi tilted his head to the side, pouting. "Hmm, not the warmest greeting I've ever had, but I expected nothing less really. From you." He cleared his throat. "Nunzia and her Pet saw your *Mo Cheann Beag* on the television. An airport in Madrid."

"An' ya were worried about ma photo in the paper," Thad breathed, rolling his eyes.

Pepi turned, looking at Thad as if he were an insect, before returning his attention to Annelie. "Does Kali know what she's doing? And with a child vampire. I knew you liked to feed on the young ones—getting back at the world for the cruel loss of your own family, I imagine that's how you justified it—but *siring* one? That's different now."

"Bridget has Kali's blessing." Annelie's voice wavered. Her eyes avoided Pepi's. "As for the child, I'd never… Shreya and Ajit have joined her cause. They—"

"Shreya and Ajit?" Pepi's face lit up. "The mythic children! How long has it been since they surfaced? Four thousand years now? They must *love* you."

She closed her eyes, pressing her fingers to them. "Why did you come here?"

Pepi smirked, clearly pleased about the discomfort he caused the other vampire. "We—my coven, I suppose you'd call it—were curious. Nunzia, especially, thought it might be an enjoyable endeavor if it involved tormenting terrorists or some such activity." His lips pursed. "Plus, I thought it might be nice to visit my first fledgling. You know how special you are to me."

"Yes, I have always felt *so special*," Annelie snapped, glaring at him. "When you held me down, forced immortality on me when all I wanted to do was die. Special, my exact thought… You didn't even have the courtesy to heal my scars before siring me."

"After all these millennia, that's still the thanks I get." With lightning speed, Pepi was beside her, stroking her back. "You deserved better than crucifixion, nailed to a wooden cross, rotting along the roadside for all of Rome to see. The scars are there to remind you of your mortal life, for you to appreciate the gift I gave you."

Thad watched as Annelie wilted under her sire's touch. The mix of terror and revulsion in her topaz eyes made his chest tighten. And, before his brain registered what his body was doing, his fist met Pepi's face, making the Ancient stumble backward.

Annelie inhaled a startled breath, covering her mouth.

Pepi cradled his nose as it healed and then shook blood from his fingers. An instant later, he slammed Thad against the wall. "How dare you lay your hands on me?" Rage burned in his eyes as he lifted the weaker vampire by the throat. "Do you know who I am? Pepi II Neferkare. I was the longest reigning pharaoh of Egypt, deputy of the gods on this earth during that time, last great pharaoh of the Old Kingdom. And you are… who? Who are you to touch me?" He banged Thad's head against the wall hard enough to dent the plaster.

Thad wheezed, the breath that had been knocked out of him returning as the bass from the music below vibrated through his body like a heartbeat. "Thaddeus P. Boyd. Kali's personal assistant." A grin turned the corners of his mouth up as a tremor went through Pepi. "Ya know Kali well, don'cha?" The Ancient's grip eased. "Didn' she run ya down in the middle a the night ta sire ya?"

Pepi bared his fangs, a low hiss escaping him as his face moved for Thad's neck.

"Get off of him," Annelie commanded, her voice steady as she walked closer. "You know Kali won't be happy if you hurt him."

Pepi slowly released Thad, letting him slide to the floor, then turned to her, running a hand over his head.

"Go. If you want to help in Bridget's crusade, I can't stop you. Take Nunzia, your little *coven*—" she spat the word "—and find her and Ajit. They're in Egypt. You'll feel right at home, I'm sure."

"Indeed." The ancient vampire straightened his double-breasted jacket. "I had hoped this meeting would be more pleasant, Annelie." He turned and left without another word.

Thad rubbed the back of his head as Annelie knelt beside him. "Thinks highly of himself, doesn' he?"

"He could've killed you."

"Yeah, well… coulda. I was more scared when I thought Livia was gonna destroy me for makin' out with her daughter."

"Idiot." Amusement laced the word.

A corner of his mouth quirked up. "I'm startin' ta think that's a term of endearment from ya."

Annelie's face softened as she shook her head at him. She gently tilted his chin up, the tips of her fangs peeking out from her parted lips.

Thad raised an eyebrow at her. She'd been adamant about not sharing her blood with him during their two years together. "Ya never… an' I don' think after…" His gaze shifted from hers.

"I don't expect you to forgive me. I haven't truly forgiven myself, but I've come to terms with who I was and what I did." Annelie bit her bottom lip. "Despite what I did and how it disgusts you, you stood up to Pepi, risked your life. Let me do this." She nuzzled his neck, then slid her teeth through his skin before he could protest.

"Shit," he breathed, a jolt of pleasure mixing with the pain. His fingers wove themselves into her hair, his teeth tingling at the thought of tasting her blood. Her hand glided up to the back of his head and eased his mouth down to her throat, inviting him to drink. Without another sound, he bit down. Dark chocolate and red wine flooded his mouth, healing his bruised body as it spread through him.

❧

Bryan Pasternak gently stroked the swell of Heidi's belly and slid out of the bed, careful not to wake her. He could tell something was bothering her; though, she only smiled and blamed her pregnancy hormones. But he couldn't get to sleep thinking there was more than she was letting on.

Closing the door gently behind him, he made his way down to the living room. Shame punched him in the stomach as he sat down at Heidi's desk and flipped open her laptop. "I can't believe I'm going to do this."

A list of recently bookmarked websites greeted him as soon as he opened her Internet browser. An author's site was the first. "Lucian Llewellyn?" His head nodded as he recognized the man. "Ah, right! He was one of the guys from the plane." He sat back in the chair and scrolled through the descriptions of Llewellyn's books. "What's everyone's obsession with vampires? And why do the authors always wear so much velvet and lace? Never knew Heidi was into that crap. Then again, who wouldn't be curious about one of the guys who saved a plane full of people…"

Curious, he clicked on the next link. " 'Dave Lives!!! Do immortals walk among us? We show you the truth!' " he read quietly, laughing at the over-the-top conspiracy theories that followed the heading. "I know she isn't falling for this stuff!"

But his laughter faded as he looked through the following sites, chatrooms and paranormal websites where people claimed they were or had met real vampires. A tremor went through him at the stories, though his brain insisted they couldn't be true: clubs where people went to drink each others' blood; psychic vampires who fed off auras; the disappearance of a reporter who supposedly got too close to exposing vampires; celebrities who the websites' owners argued were immortal for one reason or another. "What is she getting into? No wonder she's been off lately. This stuff is giving me the creeps."

As Bryan shrugged, pushing a chill away, and started to close the laptop, he noticed an open notebook next to him. He clicked on the desk lamp and skimmed over her handwriting.

> *Released his first novel in 1996. 20 yrs ago and still looks like he's—what—25. Something not right here. Can't be what's on these sites, but he looks the same as he did on his first book cover. Immortal? This is driving me crazy. And what about the girl? That other guy saved her life! I swear he kissed her or… did he give her his blood? What would that mean for us? Why were they on that plane? How do they stay hidden? What happens if I get too close…*

"I went down the rabbit hole. I'm sorry."

Bryan jumped at his wife's soft voice and turned to her. "Heidi, I-I didn't mean…"

A small smile turned her lips up. "No, part of me wanted you to find it. I don't know what to think. I shouldn't've started." She sat down on his lap and rested her head on his shoulder. "It seems like madness, but I think I'm onto something. There's just too much out there that proves it."

He wrapped his arms around her, nerves on edge thinking about the last line she had written and by what might come out of her mouth. "Tell me about everything you found…"

Chapter Twenty

Belle Hollow Bound

"… And in other news… Lindsay, did you see how yet another terrorist attack went horribly wrong?" The radio host unsuccessfully suppressed a snigger.

Lindsay replied with her whiskey laugh. "You mean the one in Cairo, Lacey? At the Khan El Khalili bazaar? Yeah, I read about it last night."

"For those of you who're in the dark," Lacey continued, "three heavily armed men wearing explosive vests entered the Khan El Khalil bazaar yesterday. They drew their guns, going—" The host performed an exaggerated war cry.

Lindsay snorted. "Be nice now."

"But… their guns jammed, and then, when they tried to detonate their vests… nada! So… The vendors and patrons proceeded to tackle them. And it was *not* as peaceful as the incident in Madrid earlier this year. Did you see the photos?"

"Oh, yeah. Mhmm. Beat the ever-loving hell out of 'em. Crazy. I guess the lesson is don't mess with Egyptians on their market day." The deejays broke down in laughter.

"Seriously, though. It's wonderful how many of these attacks are going to crap. The Air France flight, the Brussels train station, Madrid… It's like the terrorists are half-assing everything. Bin Laden's probably spinning in his watery grave."

Lacey sniggered again, but Lindsay was silent.

"Linds?"

"Sorry. I was just thinking… So weird how much these failed attacks are happening, you know? It's like—I don't know—like the universe is tired of bull."

"Whoa. Getting a little deep there."

"Yeah, well, you know me. Makes me think of things my dad and me talked about before he died. Forces beyond humans—gods, angels, whatever—getting sick of us."

There was a pause before Lacey's husky voice broke the silence. "Really philosophical now… On that note, let's hear from some of our sponsors. When we come back, let's hear from some of you out there. What's your take on what's happening? Give us a call."

☞◈☜

Cassie Lynn switched the radio station as a sign caught her attention.

Welcome to

Belle Hollow, West Virginia!

Established 1884

As she turned down East Boulevard, she slowed, taking in how the summer sunlight illuminated the tree-lined street and historic brick buildings before the marquee of Hart Theatre stole her attention. "As good a guess as any to where I could find them." She pulled into a parking lot down the block, quickly finding a spot though the main street had been full of people. She looked around but couldn't find a meter.

"Excuse me, ma'am, where do I pay?" Cassie Lynn asked a passing woman.

"No need to pay. We…" The woman trailed off, her jaw going slack as she met Cassie Lynn's face. She forced an embarrassed smile. "Sorry, um… parking's always free in Belle Hollow. Have a nice stay."

"Thank you!" Cassie Lynn replied. The stranger nodded as she walked away, glancing back quickly before entering a store. The young woman's lips lifted in amusement. "Maybe I caught her off guard?" She crossed the street, eager to see if Lucian and Thad were at the theatre.

The lobby was as empty as Cassie Lynn expected, but it didn't stop a surge of excitement from flowing through her stomach. "I've wanted to see this place for forever," she breathed, taking in the glittering chandelier above her, the veins of dark blue in the gray marble floor, and the posters from past shows decorating the walls. She shook off her awe and headed towards the box office, hoping to find someone.

A middle-aged man behind the glass glanced her way. "Be right with you." He turned back to his computer and raised his hands to type, but they slowly fell to the desk. The man rose and turned to her, unsuccessfully trying to hide a look of disbelief. "Sorry about that. I'm Aidan. H-how can I help you?"

"I didn't mean to startle you. I know theaters aren't the busiest places when it's not showtime." Cassie Lynn scanned the empty lobby. "I was looking for Livia Hart. And Lucian Llewellyn and Thad Boyd, if they're here."

Aidan nodded. "Right. Livia and Lucian aren't here. We just closed a run of *Macbeth*, so everyone's taking it easy. They'll be at Turner Books tonight—there's a band playing in the cafe. As for Thad, he left last week for business in Las Vegas."

"Oh, damn. Okay. I'll try to catch them there. I guess… I need to find a hotel." Cassie Lynn bit her bottom lip.

"There's a B and B at the end of East." He tried to inconspicuously study her features. "Tell them why you're in town. They'll take good care of you."

A corner of her mouth lifted as she realized why the man was giving her the once over. "I kinda look like Livia, don't I?"

"Well…" Aidan shrugged a shoulder. "A little more than kinda, honey. You'll probably get some odd looks from people."

"Already have." She nodded. "Thank you."

"Anytime," he answered, turning back to his desk.

Cassie Lynn laughed to herself as she walked back to her car. *This is going to be an interesting visit!*

๛๛

"… I wonder how much shite Annelie gave Thad after he…" Lucian trailed off, his eyes following Livia's as the cafe door opened. She wasn't the only one staring in that direction as Cassie Lynn entered and surveyed the room. "You knew she was coming, didn't you?"

"Yes." A corner of Livia's mouth quirked up. "I'm not sure what she's after, but, yeah, I knew." She sipped her wine. "I never go into her mind. Didn't when she was younger either. Maybe she has a thing for Thad."

Lucian's eyebrow lifted. "Oh, Christ. I knew she inherited your affinity for accents."

"Got you in the door with me… twice." Livia pursed her lips playfully.

Shreya looked away from the band. "Thad is one reason she came, but not why you think." A smile spread across her face, dimpling her cheeks. "Thad passed her his memories when he healed her. Not on purpose—he's not as able to control those things as well as the rest of us. She's here for answers about what really happened on that flight."

"Shite," Lucian breathed, seeing Livia's face fall out of the corner of his eye. "How many of his memories?"

"Quite a few. His siring, his life before and after it, healing her."

"Shite," he repeated, running a hand over his hair.

Livia tilted her head to the side and eyed Shreya, curiosity replacing the worry on her face. "How do you know?" She studied the Original with amusement.

Shreya slid a hand over Livia's. "I've been watching her since you were sired. We—the Children—watch over the mortal offspring of vampires."

"I always imagined most adult vampires kept watch over their children afterwards." Lucian took a long drink and leaned his elbows on the table. "I did."

"The watch they keep isn't always a good one," the Original said, shifting uncomfortably. "Those who weren't willing fledglings often take their anger out on the family they left behind, especially the younger ones." Lucian and Livia exchanged a loaded glance that Shreya quickly interpreted. "Not Annelie. She *never* thought about hurting her own son. It was one redeeming thing about her…"

The Original grew silent as Cassie Lynn reached their table.

"Excuse me," the young woman said nervously, though her face lit up with excitement as she looked from Lucian to Livia, "I don't know if you remember me…"

"It would be impossible to forget you, Cassie Lynn Monroe." Lucian grinned up at her and pulled out the chair next to him. "Have a seat."

༒

Cassie Lynn sat down, her nerves singing as she pulled the chair closer to the table. "I'm so sorry to interrupt your night out." She looked from Livia to Lucian, then smiled at the little girl across from her, an odd feeling of déjà vu tilting her head. *She seems so familiar. Was she at the airport with them?*

"It's no problem. Really," Lucian answered, waving a hand to a passing waiter. "Let's get you a glass."

She raised her hands. "I'm not old enough."

"It won't be an issue here." Livia met her gaze, mischief in her eyes. "What brings you to Belle Hollow?" She poured wine into a fresh glass and handed it to Cassie Lynn.

"Thank you." She took a sip, hoping to gain some liquid courage before explaining why she came. *My God, I hope they don't think I'm crazy.* "I've wanted to come here since I was, like, fourteen. My drama club advisor had visited over summer break and told us all about your production of *The Tempest.* Just... everything she said... I could never convince my parents that it would be a good vacation, though."

"I imagine not. All most people come for is the theatre or the quaint atmosphere downtown, stay a night or two, then leave for the state parks down the road." A corner of Livia's mouth pulled up. "It's a shame you missed the closing night of *Macbeth.*"

"I would've loved to have seen it!" As the conversation lulled and they listened to the band, she noticed the child studying her and moved her eyes down. *Damn, she looks familiar. Had to be at the airport with them.*

Lucian leaned his elbows on the table, bringing her out of her own thoughts. "Is something the matter?"

Cassie Lynn fidgeted. *How am I going to breech this subject? Yeah, so, I've been having some fucked up dreams and I drove six hours to ask: What the hell happened on that plane?* She glanced up at the girl, whose familiar countenance suddenly calmed her. "I... I'm curious what happened on that flight after I passed out."

Lucian nodded, his mouth quirking. "I imagine you are." He looked over at Livia. "Let's go over to the house. It's quiet there and we can talk." He pushed his chair from the table and rose, taking the lead.

The little girl hopped from her seat, gently grasping Livia's hand and offering her other to Cassie Lynn.

Cassie Lynn hesitated, then let her fingers wrap around the child's. *She is a cutie*, she mused before her nervous energy punched her in the stomach. *"I imagine you are."* Does *that mean something* did *happen to me? Do I really want to know if it did?* Her teeth grazed her bottom lip, her heart lurching, as they walked out of the cafe. *Too late to turn back now, Cassie girl!*

Chapter Twenty-One

Awe at All Angles

Bryan Pasternak sat down in front of Heidi's laptop, not sure he wanted to see any more of his wife's discoveries.

"Read through the conversations I've saved when I go to my sister's this weekend," she had instructed as she packed her bag. "I've been chatting with someone—BabyDoll—for a few months now. The things she tells me... They're hard *not* to believe. You might get to chat with her, too. She usually logs on around nine or nine-thirty. Just use my screen name."

He opened the folder on her laptop and scrolled up to their first private conversation, January tenth.

> ***BabyDoll:*** *Hiya! I've seen your name come up here for a month now, but you're always quiet in the group. If you want to talk in private, I'll be on all night. :-)*
>
> ***Heidi:*** *Hello! I know, I'm such a lurker! LOL There's so much to take in & I don't know what to*

ask… *without making myself look like a complete idiot.*

BabyDoll: *You never have to worry about that with me, Heidi. I've been around for a long time, seen a lot of idiocy in this world. But nothing you ask in your search of knowledge will make you look like an idiot to me. I promise.*

Heidi: *Oh, OK. Thank you.*

BabyDoll: *;-**

Heidi: *Where do I start? Lol*

Heidi: *My husband & I were on a hijacked plane. I saw things. Things I can't explain. The more I research, the more I'm convinced the men who fought the terrorists aren't human. It sounds crazy, but here I am, in a vampire chat room.*

BabyDoll: *Most of the people here are curious like you are. Some have had encounters, others want to.*

Heidi: *What about you? Have you had an encounter?*

Heidi: *Or do you want to have one?*

BabyDoll: *Mine changed my life.*

Heidi: *What was it like? Would you tell me?*

BabyDoll: *It was terrifying. The details are best left for another time.*

Heidi: *OK. That seems fair, since we just started talking.*

Heidi: *I hope this is all right to ask. Are you a vampire?*

BabyDoll: *It's all right to ask.*

BabyDoll: *Yes. I am.*

Bryan inhaled through his teeth as he read the last line. "Jesus." He ran a hand down his face. "Can we really believe this person?" His gaze moved up to the computer's clock. "Ten p.m. I guess BabyDoll isn't showing up tonight." He turned his attention back to his wife's file.

⁓⧫⁓

Cassie Lynn nodded, smiling at Livia as she pointed out different buildings and told her bits of Belle Hollow history on their walk, but her heart gave an uncomfortable thud and her mouth grew parched as they reached Livia's front porch. *Shit, shit...* The beautiful fieldstone house turned ominous as she watched Lucian turn the key and open the door.

The word "chumma" flowed through her head as they entered. She suppressed a snigger, glancing down at the child holding her hand. *When was the last time I thought of that word?*

Cassie Lynn made her Barbie doll dance around her Dream House, but her heart wasn't into playing.

"What's wrong?" Raya asked, tilting her head. "You look scared."

Cassie Lynn shrugged a shoulder, avoiding the other child's eyes. "I have to go to the den'ist tomorrow. When I hear Papa talk about going to the den'ist, he always talks about how much it hurts his mouth." Her lips quivered. "I don't want my mouth to hurt!" She dropped her doll and rubbed the heels of her palms into her eyes as tears rolled down her cheeks.

Raya hugged her, stroking her hair. "Shh, shh… Chumma." She kissed Cassie Lynn's forehead.

"Chumma?" A fit of giggles replaced Cassie Lynn's tears as the word rolled off her tongue. "You're making that word up!"

"No I'm not. Chumma." She kissed her friend's forehead again. "It means 'kiss' in my language. It's what my mama did whenever I was scared. If it makes you laugh, think of the word when you're scared. Chumma, chumma, chumma!" The child's lips gently touched Cassie Lynn's face, tickling her.

"Chumma!" she repeated, returning the kisses gleefully.

"Cassie Lynn?" Her mother peeked her head in through the open door, an amused grin turning the corners of her mouth up. "What are you getting up to in here?"

"Just playin' with Raya," the girl answered, turning to her friend, but the other girl had gone. Raya never stuck around when anyone else was there.

❧❧

The word ran through her head again as she stepped into the house, but she realized there was nothing to fear. Livia's house had a welcoming warmth that enveloped her. A stone fireplace greeted her from across the living room. Bookcases built into the walls brimmed with classic literature and plays. Her heels clicked on the hardwood floor as Livia and the child led her to the couch, motioning for her to sit as they did. Lucian squatted by the hearth as the three of them sat, and placed a log on the pile before lighting it.

Framed photographs of Livia and Lucian and Livia and a young man Cassie Lynn guessed was Livia's brother smiled down from the mantle and the walls. Her eyes roamed memories of parties, book signings, plays, graduations, and everyday life that Livia held dear. Her gaze came to a rest on a photo of Livia kissing her brother's cheek at his graduation. *Class of '93* the writing on the bottom of the frame read, and, though her brain took the date in, it didn't fully register it as odd. *How sad that she lost him. I can't even imagine.* She moved her gaze to the framed poster hanging near a bookcase. The words *Lady Strange's Men Summer Tour 1995* ran above a kneeling Livia raising blood-covered hands to the sky. *Such a prolific career. What a life she's had!*

Lucian rose to his feet, dusting his hands off as the fire roared to life, and sat in the chair next to the couch. "What makes you curious about that night? It's something I imagine most people on that plane have hoped to forget."

Cassie Lynn stared down at her hands for a moment before meeting his kind silver-gray eyes. "I…" *It's now or never.* "I've been having weird dreams… but I don't think they're really dreams. This is so crazy. I think they're someone else's memories. Some of them are—" a shiver ran through her "—terrifying." She worried at her bottom lip. "And in one of them, I was dying on that plane."

Lucian glanced over at Livia.

Cassie Lynn followed his gaze, but the girl's smile distracted her. *Chumma.* The corners of her own mouth turned up. *That's why she's familiar. Raya. How odd that she looks like my imaginary friend all those years ago.*

☞◦◦

What are you going to tell her? Livia silently asked Lucian, worry shadowing her face.

Christ. We don't have much choice but the truth, do we? he answered, his heart thumping uncomfortably at the thought.

She shook her head at him. *Unfortunately not.*

Lucian turned back to Cassie Lynn. "What do you remember?" He slid into the young woman's mind as her eyes grew distant.

"Sitting down with you and Thad, the conversation, the wine…" *Making out with Thad. My God, I can't believe I did that!*

"Those men coming down the aisle. Watching you and him take down the first two. Thad telling us to go back to our seats…" *The looks on the other passengers' faces: fear we would all die, wonder at who was crazy enough to take on the hijackers, admiration of them.* "After that… I can only remember the screams and crying of the others." Her chin dropped to her chest as she stared at her hands once again.

Chumma. Remember it, flowed through Cassie Lynn's head in another voice, bringing to her mind the fuzzy image of a diminutive, dark-haired girl.

Lucian's brow furrowed, then an eyebrow rose as he glanced over at Shreya. The Original avoided his gaze. *You did more than just watch over her, didn't you, Shreya?* he projected to both of the Original and Livia, a corner of his mouth quirking up in amusement. *'Imaginary' friend…*

Livia met his face with an inquisitive look before moving her eyes down to the Child next to her. *Imaginary friend?*

Well… the Original answered, meeting Lucian's eyes with confidence. *Yes. Sometimes watching over children turns into befriending them. And Cassie Lynn was a precocious child. I enjoyed her company.*

"I'm remembering right, aren't I?" Cassie Lynn's voice broke the three out of their telepathic conversation.

"You are." Lucian turned back to her.

"Then what... What am I dreaming? The things..."
They have to be memories! That last one...

Lucian inhaled, preparing himself for his task. "You're right: They're memories."

"How..." Her jaw gaped in confusion. "I didn't say that out loud, did I?" She glanced from him to Livia and Shreya.

"The truth is that you *were* dying, Cassie Lynn. One of the hijackers stabbed you." He knelt in front of her, taking her hands in his. "Thad healed you with his blood, and when he did, he passed memories to you." He let the glamour he had on her slip, letting her see his alabaster skin and jewel-like irises. "We're immortal, vampires."

Cassie Lynn squeezed her eyes closed. When she opened them, she stared over at Livia and Shreya, who had also let their masks on her mind fall away. "I... don't understand... I..."

"Yes, you do," Shreya said softly. "Your brain has been fighting it since you walked in here. The date on the photo of Livia and her brother. The one on the poster of Livia. She looks the same as she did twenty-one years ago. And me." She smiled, showing her fangs. "You know who I am. You always had trouble pronouncing 'Shreya' so you called me 'Raya.' Chumma."

Cassie Lynn pulled her hands away from Lucian's and brought them to her temples. "I..." was the only thing that escaped her lips before she fell forward, fainting into the vampire's arms.

Livia knelt next to Lucian. She pushed a lock of hair from her daughter's forehead and kissed it, and looked up at her lover. "I guess that could've gone worse."

He laughed quietly, rising to his feet with Cassie Lynn in his arms. "I'd say so."

Shreya eased off the couch as Livia stood up. "At least she's here with us. Tomorrow is a new day. She'll begin to understand."

෨෬

Bryan stretched his arms high over his head, the vertebra in his back popping in a pleasing way. He glanced at the clock. "Wow. One a.m. Time for—"

The chat room alert chimed as a private message window came up:

> ***BabyDoll:*** *Hiya, Heidi! You're on late tonight. I thought for certain I'd miss you.*

Bryan stared for a minute, not sure what he should do. "Okay, okay." He wiped his sweaty palms on his pajama pants. "Think. Sound like Heidi."

> ***Heidi:*** *Hey, gurl! Ya, late night tonite. Couldnt sleep*

There was a long pause. He winced, expecting the worst.

BabyDoll: *Starting to get nervous about meeting the little one?*

Heidi: *O, ya! Theyre nites i keep poor Bryan up w/my tossin n turnin! Lol Where you been tonite?*

BabyDoll: *I had some family things to do.*

Heidi: *Hope everthing is alright*

Another long pause.

BabyDoll: *I'm sure it will be. :-)*

BabyDoll: *This is Bryan, isn't it?*

"Crap." He stared at the screen.

Heidi: *Ya.*

Heidi: *How'd you know?*

BabyDoll: *;-) I have my ways…*

BabyDoll: *Where's Heidi?*

Heidi: *At her sister's. She told me i might be able to chat w/you while she's away*

Heidi: *:(i'm sorry i didnt tell you i wasnt Heidi*

BabyDoll: *It's all right.*

Heidi: *She had me read youre conversations*

BabyDoll: *I've been waiting for that.*

BabyDoll: *What do you think? What do you want to know about us?*

Bryan inhaled, held the breath, then let it out slowly.

Heidi: *So much more then i can even think of right now lol*

BabyDoll: *I figured that would be your answer! ;-)*

BabyDoll: *I'll start by saying: Everything I told Heidi is true.*

BabyDoll: *I'm a vampire.*

BabyDoll: *And there are so many of us living amongst you, but we're not always the monsters people believe us to be...*

Part Four

"People sleep peacefully in their beds at night only because rough men stand ready to do violence on their behalf."
Richard Grenier

Chapter Twenty-Two

A Shift in the World

Onuris scanned the faces of his comrades as Narmer explained their mission to them, his mind fighting to keep up from his recent lack of sleep.

"... after sunset. Luxor Temple will be crowded with tourists..."

The young woman from his nightmares haunted him. At first Onuris had believed she was beautiful with her creamy, fair skin, flowing copper hair, and striking green eyes. Perhaps she would be a reward in the afterlife, one of the eternal virgins to please him for waging war and changing the world in the name of their cause.

But that changed as the dreams progressed, as the woman spoke to him, spreading a dread so deep through him that he'd woken up wet from his own piss and his arms bleeding from where he'd raked his fingernails down them in terror. She was a demon like no other. A shiver ran through him as he listened to Narmer. The images she put in his mind burned.

"… This *must* go as planned. We *cannot* afford to have another incident like Cairo. Clean your weapons. Ensure that you've wired explosives properly…"

But we will continue to fail, like Cairo, like Madrid, like Brussels. Onuris longed to announce it, to tell them what the redheaded demon prophesied to him. *But, no, I mustn't. They'll think I've gone insane. I could be. She told me I am weak. I'm beginning to believe it.*

"Yafeu, Onuris…"

His head snapped to Narmer, who eyed him momentarily.

"… you will go through the crowds first. Have your weapons ready. We will follow…"

Part of Onuris pushed him to flee, but, despite the demon's prophecy, he had a duty. He knew she would be waiting for him—all of them—at Luxor Temple that evening. She had told him their fate: They would fail and die that night. They were nothing now that the world had shifted in her favor.

☙❧

Nunzia rolled her eyes as Pepi grunted yet again while he, Nunzia, and Wil passed another group of photo-snapping tourists roaming the streets of Luxor.

"Thebes turned into *this*. Nothing but ruins now." Pepi's face contorted in disgust. "And look at these people. Walking the streets as if they have any business where the kings and queens of Egypt rest. They would have been nothing in the Old Kingdom and nothing in the New Kingdom. They're still nothing. If Ramses the Great could see this…"

"Tourism is a… is the big industry here now, master," Wil hazarded, his voice shaking. He cowered as the ancient vampire glanced his way. "My apologies, master."

Pepi's eyes narrowed, but he didn't scold the man. Though he wasn't fond of humans as a whole, Wil didn't bother him as much as his other fledglings' Pets. Perhaps it was the way Wil revered Egyptian history, requesting the former pharaoh's stories with a bow. More likely it was the way the Pet averted his gaze—as he should—whenever Pepi was near. "Thebes always had a way of attracting visitors. Babylonians, Canaanites, Hittites. It was a glorious city. If the people of Egypt had done their duty to the pharaohs, the temples would have retained that glory."

"Yes, master. They did a disservice to the great land you and your successors built."

"Ugh," Nunzia groaned despite herself, sick of hearing her sire's constant complaints as they traveled through the country but knowing she had to listen or face his displeasure.

"You've something to add?" Pepi's gaze turned to her.

"Oh, no," she covered, shooting him an innocent smile. "I'm just amazed how difficult it is to find these Children." She pushed down a shudder. Children—even immortal children—made her uncomfortable. Pepi had, thankfully, offered her his gift before her oaf of a mortal husband's seed had taken root inside her womb. "The one in Cairo had been following us all night, and we didn't realize it."

They stopped short as a girl wearing rags appeared in front of them. Nunzia fought back the urge to gag as Wil grinned down. Pepi inclined his head in amusement as he had when the Child in Cairo had revealed himself to them.

"We tend to blend quite well into our surroundings." Her sparkling eyes roamed over them. "I've been sent to collect you. Ajit and Bridget are waiting."

৯৽৹

Ajit looked over at Bridget as Pepi, Nunzia, and Wil were led into the room. "You're acquainted with Pepi." The Original never so much asked her questions as stated facts.

"Unfortunately." Bridget glanced back at him, remembering her last encounter with the Ancient. "I had to kill one of his fledglings twenty years back. Pepi showed up afterward, more annoyed than angry. I doubt he's changed much. He enjoys siring and adding to his coven, I think he likes to call them." She shrugged, a smile playing at her lips as Bastien's voice flowed through her mind.

"Do you call yourselves… covens?" Bastien asked as they lounged on her balcony one summer night, sipping champagne and stargazing.

"What a random question!" She laughed. "What made you ask that?"

He took a drink from his flute. "Je ne sais pas. Don't know. Just thinking I should learn these things. I don't want to appear uninformed when I meet your friends."

She pulled herself into a sit and studied his face. "Does that mean what I think it does?" A pleased grin split her face. "You'll let me?"

"Peut être…"

"But… your family?"

"Papa always figured I'd be the bachelor uncle. He thinks I'm too much of a free spirit to settle down. I look forward to being Oncle Bastien once Félicien and Alix have children." Bastien's shoulders rose, an ornery glint in his eyes. "Me being a vampire may not be noticed."

"I've always hated the word coven," Ajit stated, sliding his leg off his chair arm, then standing to meet their guests. "Especially nowadays, with neopaganism." He rolled his eyes. "If those pseudo-witches knew half the things people did in ancient times, they'd run crying and screaming to their mothers."

Bridget nodded. "Blood rituals, berserkers, animal sacrifice, human sacrifice… Nothing like what they've turned it into today." She rose, taking her place beside Ajit as he unleashed a wave of his power toward them. Its warmth gently washed over her as she watched the trio's expressions: Pepi's cocky but amused; Nunzia's discomfort; the Pet's confusion mixed with awe.

The ragged girl stopped the three in front of her and Ajit and curtsied before departing. Ajit let his power ebb as they each bowed their heads and took a knee in front of him, Nunzia pulling the awestruck human down beside her.

Ajit glanced over at Bridget, rolling his eyes again. "You've been searching for us."

Pepi raised his head, uncertainty in his eyes. "Yes, your —"

"It wasn't a question. And I'm just Ajit. We Children aren't ones for titles. We're all on the same level here." He waved his hand. "Stand up."

Bridget pursed her lips to keep herself from laughing as Pepi's features fell in concession. *I wish Annelie could see this.*

The Ancient cleared his throat as he rose to his feet. "Thank you, your—Ajit." He bowed his head to Bridget. "This is Nunzia and her Pet, Wil." A helpless look spread over Wil's face as he lowered his eyes. "I trust you remember Nunzia, Bridget."

"Of course." *How could anyone forget Nunzia…*

Nunzia knelt beside the broken body, a banshee keen leaving her mouth. "Barnaby!" She flew at Bridget, but the Elder vampire swatted her away like a fly.

"He knew what would happen if he went through with it, with getting close to that reporter, then stalking her. Her articles could've

exposed our world. Her disappearance made national news." Bridget wiped blood from her lips. "Be glad it was a quick death. Others have not been so fortunate at Kali's request."

Pepi appeared next to her, an annoyed huff leaving him. His gaze went nonchalantly from Barnaby to Nunzia. "Clean yourself up, Nunzia. This is beyond our control."

"Wil and I saw you on television." Nunzia cradled Wil's chin like he was her favorite lap dog. "You're getting around again, Bridget. Madrid, Cairo, Luxor. At least it's not as an assassin this time… for other vampires at least." She fluttered her eyelashes. "There are still days I think fondly of Barnaby."

"There's a time and a place, Nunzia." Pepi glared at her; Nunzia winced. "Barnaby got what he deserved for threatening our secrecy. Bridget was doing her job, though it reduced our number by one… for a time." He forced the corners of his mouth up into a small grin.

She returned the smile uncomfortably. *Gods, when was the last time he genuinely did that?*

Mild boredom spread over Ajit's face as he sat back down in his chair, swinging his leg over the arm in his favorite position. "You're offering your coven—" his lip curled at the word "—to us. In our crusade as it were. Why?"

Pepi hesitated, meeting Bridget's eyes; she motioned for him to answer. "Why? Mmmm… various reasons. For me, mostly in response to the flagrant destruction of the country I had a hand in building. I watched it enough over the centuries and did nothing, though the bile rose in my throat. I feared the retribution I'd receive for meddling in human affairs. Kali's possible wrath, though I highly doubt she'd send you to an Ancient such as myself." He glanced at Bridget. "Now that I know that won't come, I'd take great pleasure in ending those who've helped and continue to help the destruction along." His lips turned up smoothly this time, sending a chill down Bridget's spine at the joyous malice in the gesture. "As for my followers, when Wil and Nunzia told us they saw you, they were eager to join the game. Their reasons may not be as virtuous as yours, but the opportunity for a little anti-terrorist fun is too tempting to pass up."

Ajit pushed out his lips as he weighed Pepi's words, then he turned to Bridget. "I'm not really fond of the thought of your coven—" a sneer spread over his lips again "—joining us but… Bridget?"

Bridget's eyes roamed over the three in front of her. *The world is shifting, bringing us all together for this.* Her stomach flip-flopped between anxiety and excitement. *What could we do all together? Could we change the world?* She met Ajit's face. "Pepi knows I'm no fan of his—" Pepi's head bobbed in agreement, but he didn't interrupt "—but this could be what we need to win in this, to put an end to radicals, to innocent lives being lost."

Ajit slowly rose to his feet. "Indeed." He looked at Pepi, Nunzia, and Wil in turn. "Don't disappoint us." He turned and left without another word.

Pepi, Nunzia, and Wil stared at him, and then at Bridget.

"He doesn't say much. But trust what little he does say: Don't disappoint us." She motioned for them to follow her, wondering what Ajit would do if they did disappoint. "There's an attack planned for tomorrow evening. I'll fill you in."

৵৽৾

Onuris's palms grew slick with sweat as the illuminated columns of Luxor Temple loomed over him and Yafeu. Carefree tourists surrounded them, clicking photographs of their friends and family. Children gazed up in awe at the stone pillars towering over them.

A chill ran down his back as two of the children turned to face him. Their eyes shared the same gem-like quality of those of the demon of his dreams. They grinned before sprinting off into the crowd. *Did they have… fangs?*

"Narmer, Ain, and Mus'ad are in place." Yafeu's voice startled him.

Onuris looked up across the temple as Narmer gave them the signal to open fire. Ain and Mus'ad let loose deep howls as they raised their guns. Tourists scattered in shock and fear as they saw the men. Panicked voices and cries filled the air.

A glint of copper hair caught Onuris's attention as he raised his AK-47. The demon stood near one of the columns, staring at him. He aimed at her and pulled the trigger, bracing himself for the kick of the weapon. But nothing happened.

He turned to his partner, whose gun had also failed. "It's not working!" Desperation spread over Yafeu's face as he dropped the magazine out of his gun and fumbled to load a new one, hopeful that it would solve the problem. A humanoid blur knocked the man off his feet before he succeeded.

The blur materialized into a man over Yafeu as Onuris watched. A satisfied smile spread over the stranger's face as it turned up towards him. He tore off Yafeu's head like the bloom of a flower and tossed it to Onuris.

Onuris involuntarily caught it, his eyes widening as he looked down at Yafeu's gaping mouth. His shock only lasted a moment though. He flew back, slamming into a column next to the redheaded demon.

The stranger pinned him to the stone by the neck. "You are a disgrace to my Egypt," he hissed, baring his fangs, then sinking them deep into Onuris's throat.

As he fought against the stranger, his vision growing fuzzy, he could see his demon walking away. *You could have saved yourself, Onuris. I gave you fair warning that this would happen,* flowed through his mind in her soft voice. *The reign of terror is ending.*

Chapter Twenty-Three

Once You Are Awake

Sinead Moss sipped her coffee as she stepped into her office. Mike Ashe sat on the edge of her desk, staring down at reports, his wide eyes moving back and forth over the papers.

"Now that's a look I never expected to see on anyone's face in this building." She sidled up next to him, set her mug on the desk, and glanced over his shoulder.

"Interpol's report from last night's Luxor attack." He handed her a stack of papers and photos. "Insane."

Sinead flipped through the photos first, understanding her partner's wonder. "How the hell did this guy lose his head?"

"The hell if I know." Mike turned his hands up and lifted his shoulders. "The official story is that the explosives he planned to detonate didn't go off properly."

She squinted down at the photo. The man's head lay next to another man, whose look of horror and fear was frozen on his face. "But… it's clean off. Like someone popped it off."

Mike picked up her mug. "You mind?" She shook her head; he took a drink. "That's what I thought. And look here." He took the papers from her and pulled out a typed sheet. "All the witnesses say there was no explosion. Not even a gunshot. Witnesses said the men raised their weapons, but they didn't go off."

Sinead pursed her lips and tilted her head towards him. "They could've just not realized there was gunfire. The stress of experiencing an attack firsthand messes with memory." She skimmed the paper. "What do the witnesses say happened?"

Her partner held up the report. "Says the men yelled, raised their guns, and nothing happened. One witness says a man came out of nowhere and attacked the guy who lost his head, then he went for the man in this photo." He pointed to the man whose face displayed eternal terror. "The other three men involved pulled out knives, but before they could attack anyone, a group of Italian tourists disarmed them."

"Jesus Christ. What did the man who apprehended the first two terrorists say?" She looked through the report for his statement.

"No one could find him when it was all said and done. Must have wanted to remain anonymous."

"I suppose it wouldn't be beyond the realm of possibility." She shrugged. "Isn't this, like, the third or fourth attack to go south since that Air France hijacking in November?" Mike nodded, taking another drink from her mug. "Pretty soon we're going to have to find new jobs." A small grunt left her. "I guess it's back to stripping for me."

Mike choked on his mouthful of coffee, his eyes widening once again.

"Kidding, Mike, kidding." She rolled her eyes, laughing. "Go get to work. I want to go through these photos." She sat down at her desk as Mike left, taking her coffee with him, and set the photos out in front of her.

A glimpse of red hair caught her attention in one of the eyewitness's photos. "That woman... Where have I seen her before?" Sinead opened her laptop and pulled up the footage from November's attack in Brussels and January's attack in Madrid. "No way... Can't be..." Her stomach cartwheeled as she remembered thinking she had seen Thad Boyd from November's plane hijacking in Alexandria and in the photos from Las Vegas. "Did I ever find those interviews with him and Llewellyn?" A long, heavy breath left her. "It's a good thing it's not time for a psych eval. I don't think I'd pass."

❧⚜

A ray of sunlight came through the sheer curtains, falling across Cassie Lynn's eyelids. She rolled onto her back, stretched, then opened her eyes. The smell of sausage, biscuits, and eggs filled her nostrils, her stomach growling in anticipation, as she looked around the room. It wasn't the bed and breakfast room she had rented for the night, yet her suitcase and makeup bag stared back at her from across the room.

"This must be Livia and Lucian's house." She sat up, her head protesting. "Goddamn. I must have drank too much." A nagging memory pulled at the back of her brain, but she ignored it as she looked down at herself. "And I slept in my clothes. Good job, girl."

Cassie Lynn slid off the bed and made her way to her suitcase, pulling out a clean pair of jeans and a sweater. She pulled her hair into a ponytail and fixed her makeup, annoyed that she'd broken her nightly face washing routine. *That next zit is all on you, drunkie.*

After a glance in the mirror, she stepped out of the room and headed down the stairs. *I hope I didn't make some kind of idiot of myself last night.* She took a deep breath as she reached the kitchen, steeling herself for any embarrassment, but neither Livia nor Lucian were there. The man from the theatre sat at the counter drinking coffee and reading a newspaper.

"Morning," he said, glancing up at her. "Coffee's over there." He set the paper down, an article about a terrorist attack in Egypt facing up.

A corner of her mouth quirked up, and she pointed a finger at him in recognition. "Aidan, right?"

"That's me." He took a sip from his mug. "I made you breakfast. Probably not as good as what the B and B would've had, but I've never had any complaints about my cooking."

"Thanks. I appreciate it." She grabbed a plate and filled it, poured herself a cup of coffee, and sat across from him.

Aidan silently studied her as she ate. "I heard you had one hell of a night."

"Yeah." She groaned. "I owe Livia and Lucian an apology for drinking so much. I wonder what they think of me now."

"I don't think that's… necessary?" His eyes narrowed in confusion, then an eyebrow rose in understanding. "You don't remember what happened, do you?"

Cassie Lynn cradled the steaming mug in her hands and stared at Aidan. "No… Yeah, I remember. We came here to talk about what happened on that hijacked flight. I…" Her eyelids slipped halfway down. "Lucian told me— *oh.*" The memories of the previous evening flooded back: what she'd been told about dying and how her companions' eyes and skin suddenly looked different, ethereal. Coffee spilled over the rim of her mug as she started.

"There it is." Aidan laughed. "It's a bit of a shock, isn't it? Learning that vampires exist. A wicked mind fuck, but you'll get used to it. And you're young, so it will be easy for you."

She stared at him, her mouth agape, her heart pounding.

"Don't worry, honey," he said, his gaze softening. "You're safe here. Livia's taken good care of me and the other humans in Belle Hollow for a long time, and she won't let anyone harm you either."

Cassie Lynn's vision blurred, but she forced herself to focus. *Do not pass out again! Life gets stranger every time you do.*

৯৽৶

Cassie Lynn smiled at a passing woman as Aidan led her down East Boulevard. The woman returned the gesture, trying to quickly study the young woman's face before the pair passed.

"Have you gotten used to the looks yet?" A deep laugh left Aidan.

"Shit no. Everyone looks like they've seen a ghost when they see my face."

"Your resemblance to Livia is…uncanny. And obviously no one is used to seeing her out in the daylight." He stopped them in front of the bookstore.

"I guess they wouldn't, huh?" Her voice dropped. "So… everyone here *knows* about…"

"Yes. Most of the residents are either Pets—constant companions to a vampire—or willing blood donors. We have a good thing going here." Aidan opened the door and motioned for her to go in. "Coffee?"

"Anything stronger?"

"You sound just like I did when I learned." He pulled out a chair for her at a nearby table and another for himself. "What can I get you?"

"Dirty chai?"

"Coming up."

Cassie Lynn watched him as he went to the counter, turning the information she'd recently learned over in her mind. *I almost died. Vampires exist. There's an entire town where they live… side by side with humans.* A breath left her as Aidan returned. She took a long sip, the liquid spreading warmth throughout her. "Um, how did you end up here? If you don't mind me asking, that is."

"I don't mind." An unreadable look glazed his eyes as he stared down at his mug. "I was, uh, homeless, a transient. It'd been that way for—" he puffed out his cheeks, then released the air "—for three years or so." He met her eyes. "I was a, uh, soldier in Bosnia. Christ, that was before you were even born." His lips lifted, and he took a drink. "I was different when I got home."

"PTSD?" Cassie Lynn whispered, her heart hurting for the man.

He nodded. "My wife… neither one of us knew what to do. I had nightmares, flashbacks. Pulled my forty-five out on her during one." His brows drew down. "She begged me to get help, but I was… too proud, I guess. I left instead. Just took off one day while she was at work." A wry laugh left him. "Stupid man that I was."

Cassie Lynn studied his face as he grew quiet.

"Anyway, I went from place to place and ended up in Belle Hollow. There were looks when I wandered into town; some were probably of worry now that I think back. There were no homeless people around, but I didn't even register that." A shoulder briefly lifted. "I found a liquor store, bought a bottle with money I had begged in my last town, and found a nice alley to get wasted in. What I did most days.

"I came out when it got dark, hoping to earn some money." Aidan's Adam's apple bobbed as he swallowed hard. "The people I saw. The humans were, of course, like you and me… but I could see the vampires among them, though I didn't know that's what they were at the time. The pale skin, the cat-like eyes. I didn't know what I was seeing. One after another looked at me, as if they knew I knew. I ran down East, screaming and grabbing passers-by, hoping to *not* see whatever my brain thought they were, but they were everywhere." He drank the last of his coffee.

"I don't remember where I ended up, but it was dark and quiet. I curled up in a ball, holding my temples. My head was on fire. A minute later, someone knelt beside me." His lips parted, but no sound came out. "Livia. She was like the others I'd seen, but there was a—" he raised his hands over his chest, palms facing him "—a feeling of warmth washing over me. Something I hadn't felt for a *very* long time. She offered her hand, telling me I was safe there, I had a home if I wanted it." A soft smile spread over his face. "She cleaned me up, found me a place to live, gave me a job at the theatre. Your—" his eyes grew wide as he stopped himself "—Livia saved me from myself."

Cassie Lynn tilted her head, momentarily wondering why Aidan paused mid-sentence but figuring emotion overcame him. "How could you see the vampires? I-I couldn't." She bit her lip.

He gently tapped his temple with his finger. "The PTSD. They hide themselves with a mask, a glamour or something, but people with mental illness can see through it, for better or worse. They had to let down the glamour to show you the truth." His hand slid over hers. "Are you okay, honey?"

She hummed, squeezing his hand. "I'm still deciding on that." The corner of her mouth quirked up. "So… are you Livia's Pet?"

"No. Livia doesn't take Pets. Occasional drinks, yes, but Pets, no."

Cassie Lynn inhaled deeply, held the breath, and released it, feeling the gears in her mind turning over her next question. "What, um, I mean, why are there so many vampires here? What's the purpose? If there is one."

"It's a safe haven for weaker vampires. One of many throughout the world. Livia is incredibly strong. She helps them, teaches them to live safely and discreetly in an ever-changing world. It's a haven for humans as well. We're safe here, no matter what our pasts were." Aidan's eyebrow lifted as he thought. "We have a great symbiotic community."

Cassie Lynn finished off her dirty chai as the information settled in her brain. "And the plane? Lucian and Thad being on it?"

Aidan gave a half-shrug. "That was a happy coincidence from what I understand. They were in Paris, with another vampire whose Pet died in the attack there. Lucian and Thad were on that plane heading back to the States."

Thad's memories flashed through her head, ending with her nearly dying on the plane. Her breath caught in her throat. "It was a good coincidence or everyone on that plane would be dead. I'd be dead," she whispered, staring down at her empty mug as tears burned her eyes.

"I know." A comforting smile spread over Aidan's face. "It's best not to dwell on it. You're alive and—my God!— the things you now know." He pursed his lips. "Mmmm… Livia told me you're going to Juilliard." She nodded at him quietly as he rose, offering his hand. "C'mon. You need a proper tour of the theatre. Livia would kill me if I didn't show you."

Cassie Lynn took his hand and let Aidan led her from the bookstore. The thought of exploring the theatre pushed her tears away.

Chapter Twenty-Four

Checkmate

Bryan could see the tears shining in Heidi's eyes. "I'm just saying we should take whoever BabyDoll is with a huge grain of salt." *And maybe a little caution,* his mind added. *How does she always know when I'm the one on the computer?*

"So you don't believe her? After everything she told me and your conversations with her." The corners of Heidi's lips turned down. "And you don't think I did all the research I could on everything she told me? Damn it, Bryan, I'm not stupid. I'm not crazy for believing this." She eased herself down on the couch, stroking the roundness of her belly. "There's just too much out there *not* to see it. Look at everything since our flight. There's more out there than we can know."

"I don't think you're either of those things. You know that." He shook his head. BabyDoll's stories were a little too detailed, a little too… something he couldn't put his finger on.

"Then what am I doing?" Tears spilled over her lower eyelids.

He sat down beside her, petting her back. "I think you want to find meaning in what happened on that flight, why we somehow got lucky when others haven't. It's comforting to think that there are creatures out there who want to help us, whatever they might be." A breath left him. "But, if there was another entire species out there, we would know. Especially if they're immortal. It's like those people who like to say Bigfoot or ghosts exist. There's no proof, only anecdotes."

She sniffled. "What about Lucian Llewellyn? His photos. He hasn't aged a day since he released his first book."

"Just good genes... and probably Botox. It's not like someone like him can't afford it. And look at all the actors and actresses who don't show their age. Jennifer Aniston's pushing fifty and looks the same as she did on *Friends.*"

"I guess..." Heidi wiped her cheek with the back of her hand. "But..."

"I'm not saying don't chat with her. Just... don't take it completely seriously. It's easy to pretend on the Internet, to play a role."

"I guess you're right." Heidi carefully pushed herself into a stand and turned to him, disappointment visible in her eyes as she forced a small smile. She leaned over with a tiny grunt and kissed his forehead. "I'm going to take a nap."

As Bryan watched her walk into the bedroom and close the door, his shoulders fell, knowing this would be a point of contention between them despite reality.

But it's a point of contention inside your own mind, too, his inner voice chastised. *You want desperately to believe it along with Heidi, but you can't. You have to think logically. You have to… But there was so much that BabyDoll said that makes sense…* He shook his head, the back and forth going on inside his brain driving him crazy as it had been doing for days.

❧

Bridget pulled her legs up on the couch where she sat and tucked them beside her while she watched Wil and Natasza play an intense game of chess. Natasza had taken a particular liking to the human, connecting with him like she seemed unable to do with most others. She thought the Child probably found him endearing, with his obsession with chess and ancient Egypt.

The vampire covered her mouth as a yawn escaped her. Her precognitive sessions had become less painful over time, but they inevitably left her exhausted. Watching the Children allowed her mind to relax and heal from the onslaught of visions she had sifted through to find planned attacks.

As Bridget watched, Nunzia slid in behind Wil and ran her fingers over his chest. He leaned his head back as she bowed to drink from his neck. His eyes closed, pain and pleasure fighting for control of his features. The vampire finished feeding, ran a finger over a fang and then the wound, and kissed the healing skin. She patted her Pet's head before joining Bridget.

Wil turned back to the chessboard, but his eyes were far away as he moved his bishop.

"Checkmate," Natasza announced, satisfaction on her face.

"Damn it." The corners of Wil's mouth turned down briefly. "Rematch?"

Bridget glanced over at Nunzia as Wil reset the board. "That was hardly fair now." She laughed without humor, trying to keep how she felt about Wil's treatment to herself. Wil and his fellow Pets were half lap dogs half servants to Nunzia and the rest of Pepi's coven. Treating Pets that way wasn't uncommon—she'd known many a vampire who did it—but she couldn't imagine treating her own that way. She'd loved the few Pets she'd taken with all her heart.

How glad I am we sent half of Pepi's coven with Children to other parts of the world. A pang of longing for Bastien and the others she had taken as Pets stabbed at her. *How very different we are in this existence. How influenced by the mortal life we had and the sire who gave us immortality.*

"He doesn't complain." Nunzia's tourmaline eyes moved over Bridget, settling on her face. "Any time you're thirsty, he's yours for the taking. I'm sure you noticed, we're very liberal with our Pets."

Bridget smiled at her and nodded slowly, knowing she never would.

"I know that look." Nunzia rolled her eyes. "You don't like how we treat them. It's not like you never shared in the Pets of others. I remember the parties you came to before Kali hired you as an assassin, Lucian tagging along." She reclined back. "Though, I doubt you would have shared your own Pet if you had had one back then."

Bridget ignored Nunzia's blatant attempt to drive her to anger. Purpose had replaced any anger she had felt in the eight months since Bastien's death. "No, I wouldn't have shared my own. I couldn't have."

The other vampire turned her head away in annoyance.

"I'm sorry about Barnaby," Bridget whispered, breaking the silence that had fallen between them. She saw Nunzia's lips tremble. "It wasn't personal, and I made it a quick death."

Nunzia swiped a hand under her eyes, rubbing away tears before they could stain her cheeks. "Don't." She stood and walked towards Wil, taking his hand to lead him away from his game.

Ajit and Pepi passed her as she and Wil left the room. Ajit barely gave her a glance, but Pepi's eyes followed her until she was out of sight. The two stopped in front of Bridget before the Original looked up at Pepi. "Is she going to be a nuisance?"

"Ah," Pepi sputtered, shaking his head.

Ajit had a way of ruffling the Ancient's cool demeanor that Bridget appreciated despite herself.

Pepi cleared his throat, pulling himself together. "I'll make certain Nunzia doesn't become an issue."

Ajit acknowledged the answer with a grunt.

"She won't become one. Old grudges die hard," Bridget said, knowing how well the Original understood grudges.

"Indeed." Ajit straightened his knit cap as he turned to her. "Where are we going next?"

"Baghdad. There's a suicide bombing planned for a late night market. It will be crowded during Ramadan." Her tiredness washed over her. "They don't even stop for the religion they claim to be fighting for. And in the U.S., California. I've already told Annelie and Thad."

"Good." The Original nodded his approval and looked up at Pepi. "This time, let's not let ourselves get carried away. We Children can only do so much to steal witness testimonies from authorities and erase memories." He walked off, joining Natasza on the other side of the chessboard.

Pepi eased himself down into the spot Nunzia had left, relaxing back and crossing his arms over his chest as he studied Ajit. "What does he have against me?"

The corners of Bridget's mouth pulled up, but she forced them back down before the ancient vampire could see. "I wouldn't take it personally, Pepi. He's not very fond of adult vampires as a whole." Her eyes flitted to Ajit, who she figured was listening to their conversation.

Pepi lifted an eyebrow at her and smirked. "He seems to like you."

"I don't know if he does." An amused breath escaped her as she thought of Ajit warming up to anyone but Shreya. "He was excited to meet me because of my abilities and of the fact that Annelie spared me as a child, but I wouldn't say he *likes* me."

"Perhaps not. Then again, perhaps he sees you as the closest one of us to a Child. You were only sixteen." Pepi rubbed his chin. "Though, part of me thinks he's a bit jealous of the life you got to lead before Annelie gave you the Blood."

Bridget noticed an odd look of introspection pass over Ajit's face as he stared at the chessboard. *He missed out on being an adult like I got to be. Romantic love, marriage, the prospect of a family...* An old ache tugged at her heart at the thought of the daughter she had lost, the perfect, tiny features of the stillborn. *He never had those opportunities. None of the Children have had them. But the things they're doing now...* "That's always a possibility."

The inward expression fled Ajit's face as he moved his queen across the board. "Checkmate."

ॐ

> **BabyDoll:** *Heidi or Bryan tonight? :-)*
> **Heidi:** *guess?*
> **BabyDoll:** *Hiya, Bryan!*
> **Heidi:** *How do ya always no? :p*
> **BabyDoll:** *If I told you, it would take all the fun away. Lol How's Heidi doing tonight? She told me she's been really tired lately.*
> **Heidi:** *Ya, tired. Went to bed all ready*

Bryan paused.

"I think he's decided to stay inside until college," Heidi joked, *rubbing the small of her back as she headed to bed before nine.*

"Wouldn't be a horrible option. Warm and quiet in there." He *rose to kiss her cheek. "Want me to come massage your feet?"*

She shook her head. "Nah, I think I just want to read some until I fall asleep."

Passing up a foot rub was unheard of. It was obvious to him that she was still upset about their conversation.

> **Heidi:** *You didn't happen to chat with her today, did ya*

Bryan held his breath, wondering if Heidi had told Babydoll about their argument. *Shit. Why am I so worried? This is a perfect stranger who likes to pretend they're a vampire online.*

> **BabyDoll:** *No…*
>
> **BabyDoll:** *What happened?*
>
> **Heidi:** *Nuthing. Just curious*
>
> **BabyDoll:** *You're not a good liar, Bryan. :-(*
>
> **Heidi:** *Just*
>
> **Heidi:** *We had an argument about some things*
>
> **BabyDoll:** *I can probably guess what those things are. I'm sorry I've caused you problems. I just wanted Heidi to find the truth she sought.*
>
> **Heidi:** *i*

"Shit." Heidi's voice turned Bryan away from the screen. She stood in the doorway, a look of disbelief on her face. "Uh, Bryan?"

"Everything all right, baby?" His mouth dropped as he saw the wet spot darkening the boxer shorts she wore to bed. *"Shit."*

"Yeah, yeah, *shit…*" Her fingers wrapped around the door frame as she grimaced.

Bryan ran to his wife, his stomach dancing and his pulse racing, and hugged her. "I got you. Come on." He carefully ushered her towards the front door, grabbing her go bag.

> **BabyDoll:** *Bryan?*
>
> **BabyDoll:** *:-) Good luck, Heidi and Bryan.*

❧

Baghdad—Counterterrorism officials in Baghdad, Iraq, are investigating what is believed to be a failed suicide bombing. A refrigerated box truck laden with explosives detonated on the outskirts of the city around eleven p.m., killing its driver and passenger, who have been linked to ISIL. Authorities believe they were planning to drive the truck into a shopping centre in the Karrada district. Lead investigator Aamir Qadir said, "The loss of life would have been immense had this attack been carried out. Hundreds of people shopping late for Ramadan would've lost their lives. I know there will be many —myself included—reflecting on this thought during this holy time."

Chapter Twenty-Five

Can't Win Them All

Eli closed his eyes, letting his body go to the beat of the techno playing in the club. *I needed this so bad tonight.* He opened his eyes to his dance partner, studying the man swaying close to him. *Definitely needed this. Tall, muscular, beautiful eyes, and—drumroll please!—Australian. Yeah, that accent.* A tingle went through his stomach.

Club Shadow was more packed than usual even for a Saturday, but Eli didn't care. He looked forward to his weekly visit. The drinks, the crowds, the atmosphere, the bodies flowing together under the colored lights on the dance floor.

He needed it even more today with the week he'd had. *Of course the ER had been crazy. Idiots with their fireworks. No matter what, someone ends up blowing a finger off.* He sighed. *And if Mom tries to set me up with one more guy from her yoga class, I'm gonna scream. I shouldn't have snapped at her, but really? Dude is more feminine than she is.*

His dance partner gave him a half smile, motioning to the bar. Eli nodded as they walked towards the front of the club. *Now… this man is what I want. Maybe I can bring him home as an example… or as a husband.*

Eli laughed at himself. *Easy now. You just met Boyd.* He glanced around the dance floor. The man of his dreams had come in with a group of people, and Eli doubted Boyd was there to find the love of his life. *Have as much fun as possible while you can.*

Boyd held two fingers up to the bartender and leaned an elbow on the bar, facing Eli. "Havin' a good time?"

"I always have a good time here. Are you in town for long?" Eli thanked the bartender as she handed him a scotch on the rocks.

"Nah, unfortunately. We're just here for a night." Boyd took a drink. "Business."

Eli studied Boyd as the man scanned the crowd looking for his companions. "Shame. We could—"

A sharp bang cut him off, making him jump. Screams rose over the music as people on the dance floor scattered.

Boyd pushed Eli towards a wall, leaning close to his ear. *"Stay close to the wall an' down."*

Eli cowered as his dance partner moved towards the panicked crowd. "No!" he screamed, his voice muffled in his own ears. He opened his jaw and moved it side to side, trying to ease the pressure in his eardrums. He watched, his heart racing, as Boyd grabbed the gunman and wrestled the rifle away. He surveyed the chaos, the doctor in him taking over, looking for any injured patrons he could help.

The feel of someone sidling up next to him turned his attention. "Get do—" Searing pain ripped through his back. He let out a gurgle, grabbing at a barstool as he slid down the wall, his legs giving way. *Fuck. That-that wasn't my lung, was it? I'm fucked if it was.*

Eli's eyes moved up, seeing one of Boyd's friends—a creamy-skinned, dark-haired woman—grab the man who stabbed him as he ran past. She lifted him by his throat, squeezing until the man stopped struggling.

His vision faded out and then came back in as the people around him moved in slow motion. *Mom… shit, Mom, I'm sorry… Mommy?*

"It's safe now, Eli." Boyd stood above him, a hand extended and the corners of his mouth lifted.

Eli coughed, a spray of blood leaving his mouth. A sigh stole the last of his breath. He wanted to move, to slide his eyelids down, anything, but couldn't.

"Shit, no." Boyd knelt beside him, searching his eyes.

The last thing Eli ever felt were hot tears falling on his face.

❦

Livia turned her head as Lucian stirred beside her. His arms slipped around her waist and pulled her close to him.

"Are you ready for this?" he asked, kissing her behind the ear.

She turned over and buried her face in his chest, groaning. "How can anyone be ready for this?"

He laughed softly. "We've gotten through the hardest part. Cassie Lynn knows she's not going mad."

"You know that's not my worst fear." Livia eased back and looked up at him. "Telling her supernatural, blood-drinking creatures exist isn't nearly as terrifying as the possibility of revealing that I'm her biological mother. She'll hate me."

Lucian rested his lips on her forehead. "Uhn-uh. She won't hate you. She's infatuated with all you've done with your life… and you gave her the life she deserved, even if she didn't know it."

She rolled away from him, sitting up on the edge of the bed and staring at her bare feet as she recalled handing her child to another woman. Tiny wings fluttered in her stomach at the thought of Cassie Lynn becoming furious at her for it. "I just got to meet her, to be close…"

"I know." Lucian swung his legs over and sat next to her. "But she won't hate you, Livia." He stood, offering her his hands. "Come on. The longer we wait, the more you'll worry."

Livia sighed, rising. "I hope you're right."

Laughter floated up to the second floor landing as Livia and Lucian started down the stairs. Warmth spread through Livia's heart at its cheerful sound.

"It sounds like Shreya is good company." Lucian grinned down at his lover. "Then again, they probably have *a lot* to catch up on." He shook his head. "Imaginary friend."

"No doubt." Livia snorted in amusement. "Shreya is full of surprises, isn't she?"

"—and Mama was convinced I had the *most* vivid imagination after that time you…" Cassie Lynn trailed off and inhaled deeply as the other two vampires entered the living room. "Hello," left her in a breath. She looked up at them, worrying at her bottom lip.

Lucian ran his hand down Livia's back as they sat, the sensation unfortunately not having its usual calming effect on her. *How can this feel so much bigger than anything?* The corners of Livia's mouth turned up as she studied Cassie Lynn. *She really does look like me. What would it have been like… Don't torture yourself.*

Shreya cleared her throat, pulling Livia out of her musings. "Cassie Lynn and I were just talking about the old days and her tour of Belle Hollow today."

Lucian glanced over at Livia as words froze in her mouth. He lifted an eyebrow at her before turning his attention to Cassie Lynn and Shreya. "I hear Aidan is an excellent tour guide. What was your favorite place?"

"I think you know the answer to that!" Cassie Lynn's joy washed over Livia. "The theatre of course. I'd seen photos but never dreamed it would be so amazing in person." She met Livia's eyes. "I love it. The entire town, really."

Say something, Lucian instructed silently, squeezing her thigh.

Livia's heart skipped. "Thank you. I've tried to make this a safe haven for… everyone."

"Aidan told me what you do here and how you helped him." Cassie Lynn's gaze roamed over Livia's face. "I never would have imagined—" her brow furrowed then smoothed "—any of this world."

The corners of Livia's mouth rose. "I never would have either, back before." Memories of Lucian revealing his secret flowed through her mind: the feeling of dizziness as his glamour lifted; his pale, cold skin; his cat-like irises; his offer of immortality. "It's quite the shock."

"That's one way to put it." Cassie Lynn returned the smile, shaking her head. "All of this. The plane hijacking. Being brought back…" Her eyes rolled to the ceiling as she fought back tears. "Thad saving my life." She glanced over at Shreya. "And to have had a little guardian… vampire when I was younger." The Original beamed as the young woman petted her hair. "It's unbelievable."

"The world is an unbelievable place at times," Lucian offered.

Cassie Lynn turned her attention to him. "I suppose it is. There are *so* many questions forming in my brain right now."

Shreya rested her hand on Cassie Lynn's thigh. "Ask us anything you need to ask. We want you to be comfortable and feel safe with us."

The young woman's gaze slid from Lucian to Livia and settled on Shreya. "Why did you befriend me when I was little? I can't imagine you just pick random children to play with, and there's nothing special about me. I was an ordinary kid."

Shreya's eyes grew wide. *I didn't expect that question,* she announced to the other two vampires.

Lucian's eyebrow lifted in amusement. *What do you plan on telling her?*

The Original shifted in her seat, panic making her fidget. *I…*

Tell her the truth, Shreya. Livia sighed, a weight bearing down on her chest.

Lucian's face fell as he looked at his lover. *Are you certain that's what you want?*

Livia avoided Lucian's face, steeling herself. "Shreya and the vampires she's created—all of whom were turned into vampires as children—watch over human children, especially those of vampires." Her heart thumped against her ribs. "You are special, Cassie Lynn. There's a reason we look so much alike. You're my daughter." She hung her head and rested the tips of her fingers on her forehead, all her energy draining as the words left her lips.

Cassie Lynn covered her mouth and squeezed her eyes shut as a heavy silence blanketed the room. Shreya laid a hand on her back, but she shook the child off, instead rising to her feet and hurrying out the front door.

"Livia—" Lucian started, but she stood without a word and made her way upstairs. His shoulders fell as he watched. He turned to Shreya, hoping for some direction, but the Child had disappeared as well. "Well then. Shite." The vampire rose and followed Cassie Lynn's path.

❧❦

Lucian found Cassie Lynn dry heaving over the porch railing. He petted her back; she glanced up at him, wiping her mouth. "Come sit and talk."

The young woman followed him to a bench and sat down next to him without a word, closing her eyes and leaning back.

The vampire studied her for a moment, a corner of his mouth rising at how much her facial expressions echoed Livia's. "Are you all right?"

She opened her eyes and raised an eyebrow at him. "Would you be?"

"Probably not." An amused breath left him before the gravity of the situation hit him again. "She didn't want you to find out, didn't want you to hate her for…" *Christ, what would be the right words here?* His head tilted to the side as he puzzled over it. *What if she didn't know she was adopted?*

Cassie Lynn sat up but stared at her feet. "I don't hate her. I'm…"

"Overwhelmed?"

"Yes." She brought her palms together and rested her index fingers on her closed lips, humming softly. "I know I'm adopted," she finally said, searching his face. "My parents never kept it a secret. They throw me an adoption anniversary party every year, to mark us becoming a family. And maybe there are times it feels bittersweet, thinking someone else didn't want me, but they told me how my birth mother wanted me to have a better life than she could provide and…" Tears glistened in her eyes. "I have had an amazing life with my family."

"That's what Livia wanted." Lucian squeezed her knee in support.

"What's weird… when I first met her, at the airport, an odd feeling went through me. Then it happened again when I stepped into this house last night." She crossed her hands, placing them over her heart. "I felt whole, like I'd found a missing piece of me. One I didn't even realize was missing. I tried to brush the feeling off, but it persisted."

Lucian wrapped an arm around her shoulders, and she leaned into him. "I think Livia would be very happy to hear that. In the years that I've known her, she's felt like a huge piece was missing in her life."

"My mama says the universe brings us to the people who are meant to be in our lives."

Lucian grinned, thinking to himself of the people who had come and gone over his nine centuries of life. "Wise woman."

ॐ⌒

"… *twenty-nine-year-old Elijah Wexler lost his life in the Club Shadow attack Saturday when three men armed with rifles and knives stormed the busy nightclub. Wexler died of a stab wound. He was a resident ER doctor at…*"

Thad forced his eyes closed to stop himself from staring at the TV behind the bar at Kali's Cabaret, but the photos of Elijah Wexler, along with the image of the man's lifeless blue eyes from the night of the attack, were burned into his brain.

Fuck me. He inhaled a deep breath and let it out slowly before opening his eyes. He swirled the whiskey in his glass and pounded it back, relishing the burn that followed it down his throat. "'Nother, please." The glass went right to his lips as soon as the bartender had finished pouring.

Annelie brushed her hand along his back before taking the stool next to him. She squeezed his knee gently. "Drinking isn't going to help." Sympathy spread over her face.

He glanced at her before finishing his fourth glass. "Ain't gonna hurt neither."

"You have a point." She motioned for a glass and the bottle, then poured whisky into Thad's and her own glass. "At least, don't drink alone." They grew quiet as the music played and the crowd chattered around them. "It's not your fault."

"It is, Annie." Thad met her face, the rock sitting in his chest growing heavier. "I got cocky. Wasn' payin' attention." His brows knitted together. "It *is* ma fault he died."

Annelie's gaze fell to her glass, avoiding the intensity in Thad's eyes. "We…" The words eluded her. "More than a hundred people lived through that because of us, *all* of us."

Thad poured another round for the both of them and turned his attention back to the television.

"… *investigators are questioning Abdul Omar, Ibrahim Salman, and Johann Abbas, who were apprehended by sheriff's deputies. The men were tackled and held by club patrons prior to the authorities' arrival..."*

Thad stared back down at his glass as the report cut to interviews with survivors, two young women appearing on the screen. "Everyone shoulda lived."

Annelie moved her hand over his free one and squeezed the fingers before a buzz turned her attention. She pulled her cellphone from her clutch, exhaling heavily as she read the message she had received. "It's Livia. You need to go back to Belle Hollow."

He rubbed his cheek. "If it's for somethin' like we jus' did, I don' know if I can right now. I——"

The other vampire shook her head. "It's not... Cassie Lynn is there."

"Cassie Lynn?" Thad furrowed his brow. "What would she be doin' there?"

"For answers," Annelie whispered. "You passed on your memories when you healed her. Livia and Lucian had to tell her about us, about vampires."

"Fuck me dead." He groaned. "I can' do shit right, can I?"

Annelie took his face in her hands. "You can blame yourself all you want for that man dying, but you know it's not your fault. We——*you*——saved so many people that night." She trapped his gaze. "And now you have an opportunity to see a life you saved up close. There is nothing more right than that, the second chance you gave Cassie Lynn." She rose. "Go get your stuff. I'll take you to Belle Hollow."

Chapter Twenty-Six

Family Ties

Sinead Moss shifted in her seat, grimacing at the pins-and-needles pricking as normal blood flow returned to her foot. *The downfall of trying to sit like a lady. I should just spread like Mike,* she mused, glancing over at her partner. He looked her way and nodded before his attention went back to the speaker, a CIA special agent from California.

"… Not that planned terrorist activities have never been unsuccessful before. Don't misunderstand me. There's always the chance that someone learns about an attack or an explosive detonates too early… or not at all." Sinead's eyes moved back up as the woman motioned to the screen behind her, the photo of a London bridge coming up. "Take for example the 1996 Hammersmith Bridge bombing, where thirty pounds of Semtex—which would have destroyed the entire bridge—failed to explode. The IRA aimed to kill and destroy but was, thankfully, unable to." The next slide showed the remains of a box truck with two charred bodies lying beside it. "It seems, though, that we've had an increasing number of failed plots since last November's unsuccessful Air France hijacking. The recent incident outside of Bagdad gives us an example of explosives detonating too early. Authorities in Iraq have decided to close their investigation on what caused the triacetone triperoxide—TATP—to go off before they were ready. Their official statement is that there's not enough of the truck to investigate. Amongst us, I think they more likely don't care as long as the perpetrators are dead." Nervous laughter echoed from the audience. "Other recently failed plots—" the agent clicked to the next slide "—have left the perpetrators luckier…"

Sinead stiffened as coppery red hair in the background of the slide caught her eye before the speaker clicked away. The young woman stood beyond the crowd, holding the hand of a blonde girl. Both seemed to be studying the scene with detachment. *What the hell? There she is…* She inhaled sharply, making Mike turn her way.

"You all right?" he whispered, leaning in.

She studied her partner's face, wondering what he would say. *He'll think I've gone crazy.* "Um…yeah. The headless guy. I forgot about that. Caught me off guard."

Mike's brow furrowed. "That stuff's never bothered you before. Are you sure you're feeling okay?"

Her gaze drifted up as the next slide filled the screen. The redhead and the child stood watching as the crowd at Madrid-Barajas Airport subdued the would-be attackers. *Am I the only one who sees her in all of these?* She swallowed hard, beads of sweat forming on her forehead as her stomach churned. "Um…no. I think with everything. Stress…" Mike nodded, not wanting to mention her separation from her husband. "I think I need a vacation after all this…"

❧

Bridget eased the wall in her mind back up and opened her eyes, sorting through the images she'd seen. She exhaled as the most prominent events floated before her, making her groan. *France again. So soon.* The vampire slid down in the chair, letting her eyelids close as the silence of the room enveloped her.

"What will it be like? When you…" Bastien asked quietly.

Bridget studied his face, seeing more curiosity than fear. Her fingers went to his cheek; he tilted his head into the caress. "It's going to be terrifying."

His hand covered hers, and he took a soft breath. "I could never be terrified of you, chère."

She leaned in close and rubbed the tip of her nose to his. "You won't be able to help it." He raised an eyebrow and pursed his lips. "You don't believe me, do you?"

"Non."

A corner of her mouth quirked up. "It starts out like my little drinks, the delicate pain, the euphoria, the desire." Her hand teased his inner thigh; he grinned. "But I don't stop at a sip. Your excitement will turn to fear. You'll feel the draw at your blood, in here." She rested her palm on his chest, feeling his heartbeat quicken at her words and imagining the feel of its constant rhythm next to her for eternity. "You'll fight, your survival instincts taking over as you feel your body dying."

Bastien inhaled sharply. "Merde." His hazel irises darkened. "The entire time?"

"No." She watched his face relax. "I'll slide into your mind, talk to you, make you feel safe."

Tears burned behind Bridget's eyelids. *But I didn't keep you safe before it happened.* She blinked, meeting Ajit's quiet amber gaze.

"Did you ever tell him what he'd experience when you gave him your blood? The change?" He lounged in the chair next to hers, studying her with his usual blasé air. "You had that look on your face again."

She shook her head at his intrusion, both amused and frustrated by the Original. "I told him everything."

"I'm impressed." He slung his leg over the arm of the chair. "It seems most of you don't fully disclose what to expect, like they'll not want immortality anymore."

"Some probably wouldn't want it if they knew the pain they'd have to endure. Do you warn the children you sire?"

"Shreya and I have always believed in full disclosure. And children are resilient, more so than adults."

A soft laugh escaped Bridget, eliciting an odd look from the Original.

"I said something humorous?"

Bridget bit her lip, thinking carefully before she spoke. "Your lack of faith in adults—vampire and human alike—amazes me at times, Ajit. I imagine you had some kind of faith once. In your family when you were a human. In your aunts and father when you were turned. What happened to it? It couldn't all be Kali's fault."

Ajit's mouth opened, but no sound came out. He pursed his lips in thought, his brow furrowing. "It wasn't just Kali who killed it, no." His head tilted, and a wry smile dimpled his cheeks. "I had faith in Devika and Vivek when my mind was still foolish and young. They condemned Kali's actions yet, after a few hundred years, saw themselves as gods just like she saw herself. They abhorred the thought of giving humans the Blood but took Pets who worshiped them and offered their lives freely." Contempt flashed in his eyes. "Shreya and I watched all this, our disgust growing as our minds matured."

Bridget studied his face as he paused. "Did you try to talk to them?"

"We did, but do adults ever listen to children?"

"Sometimes," she replied, remembering how Étaín and Annelie had listened to her daydreams, nightmares, and worries when she had been a child.

A doubtful grunt left his throat. "Devika and Vivek gave our concerns very little thought. We were children, not equals, despite being just as powerful as they. We knew nothing. Our opinions didn't matter. Shreya was heartbroken at what her mother had become, and all I could think to tell her was 'Power does awful things to people, cousin. Remember Aunt Kali.' " A brief, lopsided smile turned a corner of his mouth up. "I'm sure you realize Shreya couldn't accept that answer."

Bridget nodded. "Shreya doesn't seem like the type to take things lying down. What did she do?"

"She sired a Child. The daughter of one of her mother's Pets, who had abandoned her family for Devika's... cult, if you will." Ajit stared off in the distance. "Shreya brought the newly sired Aarti to our temple, quite pleased with herself. Devika and Vivek, on the other hand, raged. How dare she give such a gift to a human and child no less? What was she thinking? Did she see herself as Kali saw herself?" He met Bridget's eyes, admiration for his cousin filling his. "Shreya said nothing, just sat with Aarti telling her how her life would be from now on. Devika grabbed her and threw her across the room. 'How dare you ignore me? *I am your mother.*' I can still hear her voice…" A shiver ran through him. "But the look on Shreya's face…"

Bridget balled her hands in her sleeves as the chill passed on to her, recalling the destruction she'd witnessed over the centuries when vampires struggled for power over one another. *A clash between Originals. I can't imagine.* Goosebumps moved up her back at the thought.

"Shreya dusted herself off and stood before Devika, quietly gazing up. In a flash, she raised her hand and Devika flew across the room, the wall crumbling down on her. 'I've had enough, Mother.' Vivek moved towards her, but it only took her turning her attention in his direction for him to stop. 'Spoiled brat. You've been given everything. And you, son?' he spat at me." Ajit's head moved back and forth slowly. "I said nothing but took Shreya's and Aarti's hands, and we left."

"I imagined much worse happening." Bridget let out a breath.

"Devika and Vivek knew better." The Original lifted a shoulder briefly. "Plus, Shreya isn't fond of violence, though she realizes it's a necessity in this world."

"It is. And, unfortunately, we do a great deal of it." The faces of the terrorists she and the Children had killed rolled through her mind. *Should I feel guilty for what I've done?* She shook the thought off, raising her eyes to Ajit. "After all these millennia, you never found anyone to renew your faith in adults?"

A dry laugh left his mouth. "Never. Adults spew hatred based on race, sexuality, and religion. They start wars over their stupidity. Look at what we're dealing with now." His lip curled, revealing a fang. "What are all these people fighting over, killing each other over? Some random god— like Kali, Devika, or Vivek—they believe in? What's the point?" His frustration washed over Bridget. "Children… we're not like that. We don't care about your religion, your bed mates, the color of your skin… until an adult tells us we should."

Bridget studied him. "You're not wrong," she whispered, her voice cracking.

"I hate having to fight alongside all of you in this war."

"I know you do." Her stomach churned.

"What's worse… Pepi was right about something regarding me." Ajit met her gaze, his eyes narrowing. "You had things I was so close to having as a human. If the rakhas hadn't attacked us, I would have had a wife and a family. I would have understood and felt romantic love. I'm trapped in preadolescence, never learning about those things or ever maturing to that point of understanding them." He pouted. "And I'm torn. I want to hate you, Bridget. Hate that you weren't much older than I was when Annelie gave you her blood but got to have those things.

But...I envy you more." He turned away in embarrassment.

Bridget's jaw slackened at his confession. "I-I—"

"Don't." A corner of his mouth quickly pulled up, then dropped back into his usual expression. "I don't like the self-reflection I've been doing with you around, but I can't blame you for it. We won't bring it up again." He gently swung his leg back and forth. "Where do we need to go now?"

She shook her head at how definite his dismissal of his envy was. "France."

"France? Here I thought we would get farther into the Middle East." A shoulder lifted and dropped. "Will it feel good to return to your home?"

"No." A frozen hand wrapped around her heart.

౿ఞ

The beeping of monitors had finally become background noise to Bryan. He stared down at Heidi, a boulder in his chest. Though she slept—exhaustion finally overcoming her sorrow and worry—tears slid down her pallid cheeks. Dark circles rimmed her eyes. His hand went to hers, his thumb running over the IV tube there.

"I'm sorry, Heidi. I'm so sorry."

Images from the night before rushed through his brain: his wife's contractions nearing, driving to the hospital, the joy on her lips, then... the look of fear on her face, doctors rushing to deliver the baby as his heart rate dropped dangerously.

Heidi let out a pained sigh, murmuring in her sleep. Bryan stroked her hair, wishing he knew the words to say to her when she awoke.

A soft hand rested on his arm, and a stab of anguish went through him. *The baby...* But, instead of a doctor or nurse, the large, innocent eyes of a young Indian girl met his. Relief washed over him, and a choked sob escaped his mouth. "I... how did you get past the nurses?" His lips parted in confusion, his tired brain not questioning her identity.

An enigmatic smile spread across the child's face. "I'm very good at sneaking around." Her head turned towards Heidi, and she gracefully lifted herself onto the bed, not disturbing his wife. She took the sleeping woman's hand and squeezed it gently. "She'll be all right."

"No," Bryan said, not realizing the child hadn't asked a question but made a statement. "She's... the baby..." He remembered the blue tint of the baby's skin, the look on the doctors' faces as they worked to get air into the newborn's lungs, Heidi's confused cries, all the blood she lost. "He might—" he took a deep breath, readying himself to say the word for the first time "—die." A flood of tears ran down his face. "All she ever wanted was to be a mother, for us to be a family. Her heart's broken… And I can't do anything."

The girl slid off the bed and embraced him. "No, Bryan, your son won't die. Heidi will be a mother." She stepped back, turning again to the bed.

Bryan stared at her. "How do you know our names?"

"You always wondered how I knew it was you using Heidi's screen name." She glanced back, raising a mahogany eyebrow.

"BabyDoll?" His heart skipped a beat. "But… you…"

"Your grammar and spelling are awful compared to Heidi's, you know."

"I know. She tells me all the time." He laughed nervously. "But… I didn't expect you to be a child. Why are you here?"

"I'm five thousand years old, one of the first vampires." BabyDoll wiped the tears from Heidi's cheek with her thumb. "I haven't spoken to my own mother in a very long time, and Heidi's been so wonderful to talk to, even if we never met in person." She studied Bryan silently. "I knew something was wrong when she didn't post photos."

The girl grinned at him, revealing her tiny fangs, then ran her index finger across one. With a finger of her other hand, she gently pushed down on Heidi's chin, and dripped blood into the woman's mouth.

Bryan listened, his stomach dropping, as the heart monitor's rhythm slowed for what seemed like an eternity, and then returned to normal as Heidi sighed. The corners of his wife's mouth rose briefly as she relaxed back into sleep. "What did you do?"

"Healed her and your son. She'll barely remember her pain, and he'll be healthy." BabyDoll kissed Heidi's cheek and turned to Bryan, planting her lips on his cheek as he sat stunned. "I should be going now." The girl made her way towards the door.

"Wait!" Bryan stood up, his mind trying to catch up with everything he'd witnessed. The vampire stopped and looked back. "We don't even know your real name. And…" *My God, what does she want in return?*

"Shreya." She shook her head. "I don't need or expect you to repay me. Just keep what you've learnt about us quiet, as you have been. The world wouldn't handle a discovery of vampires very well."

The man watched her disappear through the door before turning to his wife. He released a slow breath and reclined on the bed beside her, resting his head on her breast and falling asleep.

Chapter Twenty-Seven

Of Men and Monsters

Sinead Moss sighed as the sip of Sauvignon blanc cooled her. The streets of Marseille buzzed with tourists and residents alike on the warm evening. A corner of her mouth turned up as she watched them and listened to snatches of their conversations as they floated to her.

"*… une autre boiteille du vin, s'il vous plaît…*"

"*Bonsoir. Ça va?*" followed by kissing.

"… I love this place! I wish we could stay forever…"

"This is what I needed," she whispered, her shoulders relaxing. She let her eyelids slip partway down, leaning back in the cafe chair. *Not thinking about headless terrorists, not thinking about the next attack… not thinking about—say it, Sinead—divorce.*

The grinding sound of metal on metal from down the avenue ripped her from her meditation. Screams reverberated off the buildings as people ran from the accident.

A surge of adrenaline lifted Sinead to her feet. She grabbed the arm of a frantic tourist running by. "What happened?"

The woman wriggled her arm away, primal fear widening her eyes. "They-they rammed cars. They have knives!" She continued her frenzied dash down the street.

Sinead moved as if she was in a dream, her limbs heavy as she moved toward the place others were fleeing. She saw another car ram a parked police cruiser and two men rush out, knives held out in front of them as they joined their co-conspirators on the street.

People scattered, parting around her as she continued on her mission to help. She scanned the scene as she went, hoping to figure out where she could be of use. Her head snapped to the right, a breath catching in her throat, as a man grabbed one of the terrorists as he headed towards her, twisting the attacker's head until it popped. The stranger met her gaze, grinning as he moved on. A group of children surrounded another terrorist, moving in like a pack of wolves despite him threatening them with his weapon. Sinead's mouth gaped as the children leapt upon him without fear. Another attacker ran for them but flew through the air as if caught by a gut punch before he could reach them.

"Wha…"

And there, amid the chaos, stood the redheaded young woman and the blonde child watching from across the street. Sinead sprinted towards them, ignoring the threats surrounding her. "It's you," she breathed as she reached them. "You."

The young woman's head tilted up towards her, a lock of coppery hair falling across her pale cheek. Her lips parted as if to say something, but Sinead didn't hear what. Blackness conquered her vision.

≈◈≈

Disappointment clouded Cassie Lynn's face as she pushed food around her dinner plate.

Lucian poured her another glass of water and touched her hand. "Livia will be up to talk. I promise. This is—"

"Difficult. *Really* difficult. Trust me, I know." She smiled weakly at him, letting out a breath. Her fork *tinged* as she set it down on the plate. "I, um, I'm thinking of heading out maybe the day after tomorrow. I really should be getting back."

He nodded. "Of course. I'll—" A knock at the front door turned their attention. "Be right back."

Lucian's eyebrow rose as he opened the door to Thad and Annelie. "I didn't expect to see you two again anytime soon." He moved aside to let them in, noticing the dejected shadow on Thad's face.

"Don' even ask, mate," Thad mumbled as he saw Lucian's look.

"Rough couple of nights." Annelie's fingers brushed Thad's arm as he walked by on his way to the living room. "Livia texted me about Cassie Lynn. She thought it might help the girl since…"

"She's taking everything extremely well. But, really, it couldn't hurt." He lifted a shoulder.

"And she's sweet on Thad, isn't she?" Annelie grinned, her lip ring glittering in the low light.

A corner of Lucian's mouth quirked up. "Slightly." He studied the other vampire a moment, realizing she didn't have the same annoyance in her voice when she said his name. "You two…"

Annelie shook her head, turning to where Thad sat with his chin resting in his palm. "Nothing like that. Just friends again. Where are Shreya and Livia?"

"Shreya, the little shite, disappeared last night without telling us where she was going." Annelie gave Lucian an amused huff. "Livia's in the basement. She locked herself down there after she told Cassie Lynn the truth." His face fell, the helplessness he felt at not knowing what to do for his lover hitting him.

The other vampire squeezed his hand. "Go get Cassie Lynn. Then we'll see if we can get Livia out of her own head."

Sinead's head throbbed as she came to. She rolled to her side, gagging and heaving over the edge of the bed as her stomach protested the sudden motion. Tears blurred her vision, but she could make out two human forms sitting in front of her: the redhead and the blonde girl. She eased herself onto her back and rubbed the heels of her hands in her eyes to clear them. With a groan, she pushed herself up to sit against the headboard and slowly turned her head towards the couple.

A chill raced down her spine as she studied them. Their skin was as porcelain perfect as the dolls she'd had when she was a child, and the redhead had pale traces of freckles across her nose. Their irises reflected the dim light of the room like a cat's would and betrayed their youthful appearances.

"You're going to have a headache for a time, Sinead," the redhead said, her lips briefly lifting, "but that will be the worst of it." She reached over to a basin of water on the bedside table and wrung out a cloth, reaching toward Sinead's forehead.

The urge to claw her way through the wall behind her hit Sinead, but she sat trembling in place instead as the young woman brought the cloth to her skin. "I-It's you."

A small, kind laugh left the redhead. "You said that on the street. Who do you think I am?" The ghost of an accent floated through her words, but Sinead couldn't place it.

Sinead's brow furrowed. "I-I dunno. You're in the photos... from all the failed attacks. No, not all. Lots of them. That guy from the plane is in some, too. What's it? Thad Boyd." Her hands went to her temples.

The two turned and looked at one another.

Why do I feel like they're talking about me without saying a word? Her gaze went between them. "How do you know my name? Where am I? Who are you?"

"You're under Fort Saint-Jean. It's where we stay in Marseille," the child answered, a faint Eastern European accent lacing her voice. "I'm Natasza."

"Bridget." The woman's eyes roamed over Sinead's face. "I went into your head while you were unconscious and learnt who you are. We were worried when you approached us on the street." She laid the cloth back in the basin. "My apologies for knocking you out, but I had to be sure you weren't a danger to us... or yourself."

Sinead shook her head, aggravating her headache. "Oww... a danger to you... you knocked me out... went into my head..." She inhaled deeply, trying to wrangle the herd of thoughts in her mind. "Okay, okay... that doesn't make *any* sense."

Bridget reached out and laid her hand on Sinead's. "I know you see that we're different. We didn't bother masking ourselves. I felt your fear, the urge to flee when you realized it." She smiled softly. "We're vampires. And we have a proposal for you."

Sinead's chest tightened as she noticed the sharp fangs where Bridget's eyeteeth should be. Her hands clamped over her mouth, and she squeezed her eyes shut as she felt the scream building inside her. *I'm going crazy. Vampires don't exist. Oh, God, I'm crazy. This isn't real. This can't be. I'm having a mental breakdown. That has to be it.* Tears ran down her cheeks as she opened her eyes to the creatures in front of her, creatures that could easily kill her despite their beautiful, innocent faces.

"You're not crazy, Sinead. Please listen."

"Please stop going into my head," she choked, pushing down her terror as she moved her hands from her mouth. Tremors ran through her.

"Fair enough." Bridget's face softened, her Cupid's bow lips pursing gently. "You've seen Thad and Natasza and I in photos. That means we've not been as careful as we should have been or thought we were." A heavy sigh left her. "With your help, we could—" her head tilted to the side as she studied Sinead "—fix that."

"Fix what exactly? What are you doing at these terrorist attacks?" The words came out faster and at a pitch higher than her usual. She grimaced.

Natasza grinned. "Making certain they fail of course. Too many innocent lives are lost."

Manic laughter slipped from Sinead's mouth; the pair watched her quietly as her fit ended. "But you're vampires. Don't you kill innocent people? Feed off of human blood?"

"We prefer—" Natasza motioned around her, making Sinead wonder how many of them there were outside the room "—to feed from the less than innocent. Rapists, child molesters, human traffickers. Terrorism has long been a pet project of ours, however."

"And you can help," Bridget added. "With your position in the FBI, you can make certain we're not discovered. Get rid of photographic evidence, change witness testimonies…"

"Let vampires be judge, jury, and executioner." Sinead ran her fingers through her tangled hair, afraid of the words she knew were going to leave her mouth. She inhaled a breath, held it, then released it slowly. "What you're doing is vigilantism. I took an oath to uphold the law, not allow what you're doing, no matter what the cause." Calm washed over her as she accepted her fate. She fought back fresh tears as she met Bridget's eyes. "I'm sure I've just signed my order of execution, but… I can't."

Bridget avoided her gaze, disappointment and exhaustion clear on her face, as another vampire, a teenage boy, stepped from the shadows. "Then we're sorry," the boy said, pushing a lock of dark hair underneath his knit cap.

The world before Sinead faded to nothing.

అ❖ఱ

Thad closed his eyes and pressed the pads of his fingers to them gently. The images of Elijah Wexler were persistent buggers, creeping into his mind as it would wander to mundane thoughts. Not even the fresh air caressing his skin as Annelie flew through the sky could banish them for long. Though he'd only known Eli for an hour, he knew the man was a good, caring person. One the world desperately needed. "Senseless. Goddamn, mate. I'm sorry."

"Thad?" Lucian's voice broke him from his reverie.

He grunted as he opened his eyes to the other vampire and Cassie Lynn. A nervous laugh left his lips as the young woman studied him. "Look a bit different than ya remember, don' I?" He pushed himself to his feet.

Cassie Lynn inhaled sharply, nodding, and walked over, wrapping her arms around him and laying her head against his chest. "Thank you."

Stunned, Thad looked up at Lucian for direction, the other vampire walking away with only a tilt of his head, and returned the embrace, petting the woman's hair. Calm flowed through him at the feel of her warm body against his. *You have an opportunity to see a life you saved up close. There is nothing more right than that,* Annelie's voice ran through his brain. The corners of his mouth lifted briefly at the memory of her coming back to life in his arms on the plane. He bowed his head, breathing in the scent of her honey shampoo, and let tears he hadn't realized were building to fall. "You're welcome."

Chapter Twenty-Eight

Fear and Loathing

Livia glanced up as she heard the basement door open, and then went back to staring at her hands. She knew Lucian had tried it a few times, and she had unlocked it that evening, finally feeling like she had gathered her thoughts into a coherent thread.

"Livia?" Annelie sat down on the arm of the couch and stroked her hair as Lucian sat beside her and rested his hand on her leg. "Hey."

"Hey," she answered softly, letting out a long breath. "Thank you for coming, Annelie." Her head tilted up toward the other vampire.

"Of course." The corners of Annelie's mouth turned up briefly. "Thad needed to get away for a while after… and seeing Cassie Lynn—someone he saved—will be good for him. It sounds like she'll be happy to see him, too."

Livia nodded, turning her attention back down.

"Cassie Lynn would be happy to see you as well." Lucian rested one of his hands over hers.

"I—" Her voice cracked. "I-I want *so* badly to, but—" she rolled her eyes up, fighting back tears "—I don't think I deserve to see her." Annelie and Lucian looked at one another, and Livia got up, walking to the other side of the room where she had tortured the plane hijacker. With the toe of her boot, she traced circles on the tile, remembering the crack of his fingers as she broke them.

"That's mad, Livia," Lucian said, his voice lilting. "Why would you think that?"

"No. It's not at all. When I came down here, there was so much I wanted to say to her… but as I sat and thought how to get it out… I realized I don't deserve to see her." She turned back to them, leaning against the wall. Her stomach rolled. "Because of all this. What I did here. Torture. This is why I can't see her." She slid down to the floor, her knees bent. "How can I bring her into this life? How can I face her, knowing that I can be a monster? Knowing? Fuck… I *knew* I was a monster. You told me what we are before you sired me, Lucian. And I agreed to it. I—we—all pretend so well, don't we? But we're predators. We take life—human life—to survive. Monsters." Tears spilled down her cheeks as she bowed her head. "Cassie Lynn doesn't need to know a monster like me… and I sure as fuck don't deserve any love she could ever have for me."

Silence hung like a blanket of fog, filling every inch of the room.

"That's bullshit," Annelie whispered hoarsely. Shame and sadness fought for control of her face. "I know what it's like to *actually* be a monster. To not care about anyone or anything, not even yourself. To not care whose life you take." Her voice cracked. "And what you're doing here… it is *so far* away from making you one."

Livia covered her face, quiet sobs wracking her body. "I —" She choked.

Annelie moved to Livia, cradled the other's cheeks in her hands, and gently tilted her face up. Livia's hands fell away as Annelie's thumbs wiped away the tears. "No. Don't give me excuses. I know you better, Livia, and so does Lucian. You're scared." Lucian nodded over Annelie's shoulder, an eyebrow lifting and a corner of his mouth quirking. "You have a chance few of us ever get in this existence. You can reclaim someone you lost. To protect them. To be loved by them." Her fingers slipped down Livia's face as she fell back, sitting on her knees. "I can't even imagine what that would have been like."

Lucian wrapped an arm around Annelie, pulling her to his chest, and reached his other hand out to Livia.

Livia moved closer, leaning her head on his free shoulder. The familiar fragrance of oranges and honey and the feel of his muscular form eased her heart.

"Cassie Lynn wants this and so do you. Will you come upstairs?"

Livia relaxed against him, exhaustion taking over. "Yes."

❧∽❦

Cassie Lynn released the hug, stepping back from Thad. She reached up and brushed his cheek, studying the red tint left on her fingers from his tears. "You cry blood? Are you all right?"

"Yeah, we cry blood. Rough couple a nights." Thad ran a hand down his face, wiping away the rest of the tears. He shook his head to clear his mind. "I heard ya got some of ma memories."

The woman pursed her lips gently and sat, staring down at the coffee table in front of her. "I… I thought I was going crazy."

Thad eased himself down beside her. "I'm sorry, Cassie Lynn. I'm not as strong as the others. I guess I couldn' control passin' 'em on when I gave ya ma blood. Ya wouldn' a remembered anythin' if Lucian had healed ya. I shoulda let him do it while I took on the cockie."

"Cockie." A bright smile spread across her face as she repeated the word, trying to mimic his accent, then she looked at him, growing serious again. "Don't be sorry. I'd be… I wouldn't be here, learning about this amazing world or who I am if you hadn't given me your memories." She took his hand and placed it between her breasts. "You gave me my life. I saw it."

Thad stiffened, the gentle thump of her heart beneath his palm bringing him back to the night on the plane. He closed his eyes, remembering it in minute detail: the sounds of her labored breathing; the blood slowing in her veins; the smell of her terror; the taste of his own blood as he bit his tongue; and his fear as she lay heavy against his chest. A relieved breath left him as he relived her coming to life in his arms.

The life ya saved. Eli Wexler's dead blue eyes invaded the backs of his eyelids. *And one ya didn'.* A tremor ran through him as his eyes popped open.

Cassie Lynn took his hand in hers, brushing the pad of her thumb over his knuckles. "What's wrong?"

"I… can' save everyone and keep rememberin' a person I couldn' save."

The young woman's head tilted to the side as she studied him. "From the plane?"

"No, ya were the only one on the plane." His skin tingled at the feel of her warm fingers touching his, easing some of his ache. "From that nightclub attack in California.

I wasn' payin' attention, and he got stabbed. I didn' have time ta heal him."

"You were there as well? I know you and Lucian were only on my flight by chance… But that's really bad luck to experience two terrorist attacks."

"Not by chance this time…" A corner of Thad's mouth quirked up. "Livia and Lucian didn't tell ya what we're doin'?"

Cassie Lynn worried at her bottom lip. "Um, well, we talked about what happened on the plane, they told me about vampires… I found out Shreya was my imaginary friend when I was little and Livia is my biological mother." Her smooth brow furrowed.

"Shreya was your imaginary friend?" His eyes widened. "Fuck me dead. I missed a lot. Sounds like there was no time ta tell ya about other thin's then."

"Other things? Those things weren't enough?" Her jaw dropped, her violet eyes getting big.

Thad laughed quietly. "We're fightin' terrorism, tryin' ta save people." He squeezed her hands. "Let me give ya the rundown."

જીજી

Bright light invaded Sinead's world; she turned her head to escape.

"Madame Moss? Madame? Can you hear me?" A woman in scrubs materialized as the blinding light disappeared, a friendly look spreading over her face. *"Bonjour."*

A noise unrecognizable to Sinead came out of her mouth as she tried to speak.

The nurse nodded and raised the head of the bed so Sinead was propped up. She touched Sinead's lips with a straw. "Drink. You're probably parched."

The first sip felt like manna from Heaven. She grabbed for the cup, but the woman held it back. *"Non, non…* not too much too fast. You'll be ill."

Sinead swallowed and took a breath before relaxing back onto the pillow. *"Merci."* She closed her eyes trying to remember what had happened, but only vague images came to her and then slipped from her reach. "How did I get here? What happened?"

"You fell and hit your head last night, during the terrorist attack. There's no permanent damage, and you should make a full recovery."

Memories trickled back: the peacefulness of the evening broken by the crunching of metal; seeing people fleeing as men armed with hunting knives ran through the crowd; running towards… *What? What the hell was I thinking?*

"You were very brave, a hero. As others fled, you wrestled an attacker down. Another man knocked you to the ground where you bumped your head, but a bystander came to your aid." The nurse handed her a newspaper. "Thank you."

"I…" Sinead scanned the photos and headlines. "I was on vacation."

The nurse smiled and shrugged. "Terrorists rarely pick good times to attack, *non?*"

Despite her weakness, Sinead broke down in laughter, the other woman joining in. "This is true." She groaned as exhaustion set in.

"Rest now, Madame Moss. Your husband is on his way over from the States to bring you home."

Sinead grimaced. "Soon-to-be ex."

The nurse looked at her with sympathy, nodding, and touched her hand. "Rest… And *merci*. You are a hero to us here in Marseille."

∂∘∢

Livia stood in the doorway to her living room, watching Cassie Lynn and Thad. Her daughter's eyes were bright with excitement as the vampire described to her what they'd been doing to carry out Bridget's plans.

Thad glanced up, finally realizing Livia was there. "Hey," he breathed. "How lon' ya been there?" Cassie Lynn followed his gaze, her lips turning up.

"Not long," Livia answered, walking into the room and sitting in an armchair. *Mind if I have some time?* she asked him silently.

Thad nodded, turning back to Cassie Lynn. "I should probably give ya two some privacy. I'll see ya before ya leave."

Cassie Lynn pulled him down as he rose and kissed his cheek. "Thank you again."

Thad's eyes moved sideways, gauging Livia's reaction to the kiss.

Livia rolled her eyes, laughing quietly at the look of worry in the other vampire's eyes. *You're safe, Thad. I promise.*

He winked at her as he returned the kiss and left the room.

"So…" Livia started, the words escaping her.

Cassie Lynn fidgeted. "Thad was telling me what you've been doing. That's…I don't even know… incredible. But there's been a lot of incredible in the last few days." A light eyebrow rose as she studied the vampire. "I…" She inhaled deeply, releasing it slowly. "How do we begin?"

Livia moved from the chair and joined Cassie Lynn on the couch, taking the woman's hands. "However you want." A soft chuckle left her.

Her daughter returned the chuckle. "Shit, I want to know so much, but I don't know what to ask first. All of my questions seem both important and stupid at once." One of her shoulders lifted as her eyes moved to the ceiling. "Is Lucian my father? I guess I should have asked him that."

Livia shook her head. "Vampires can't have children like humans can. Lucian's over nine hundred years old."

Cassie Lynn's lips formed an O. "Wow, okay." She closed her mouth and pursed her lips, mulling over the information. "I'll save the question of my biological father for another time. So you haven't been a vampire very long then."

"Only eighteen years. Lucian is my sire, the one who gave me the Blood." She watched Cassie Lynn's face as the young woman absorbed the information, remembering the days she used to watch her through other people's eyes to see her learn and grow.

"There's *a lot* I want to know about that, but I hope we'll have time to talk about it another time." Cassie Lynn's gaze locked on Livia's. "Why—I guess, what I want to know is—why didn't you come talk to me after you told me you were my biological mother? You hid. Why?"

Livia swallowed hard. "I didn't think you should be around me. What I am… things I've done in the name of this war we're fighting. I've done horrible things, Cassie Lynn. On top of the normal ways vampires survive. I've tortured terrorists, *people*… and almost liked it."

Cassie Lynn's mouth opened, then closed again. " 'People sleep peacefully in their beds at night only because rough men stand ready to do violence on their behalf.' "

"Orwell?"

"No, it was actually Richard Grenier writing about Orwell." Cassie Lynn cocked her head to the side, worrying at her bottom lip. "When my dad was still a state trooper, he, um, had to shoot someone, kill them. My parents tried to keep it from me—I was only six—but it was everywhere. The man he shot was a violent piece of shit, a drug smuggler human-trafficker, probably would have murdered my dad or any other cop given the chance, but Papa was beyond upset by what he had to do."

Livia shifted, thankful she had given her only child to good people but uncomfortable by how few times she's felt anything but the warm rush of life from draining the blood from the worst of the worst.

Cassie Lynn sensed her discomfort. "What you and Lucian and vampires do has got to be different. You're not human anymore. I want to know you even if you feel like you don't deserve it." She stroked the top of Livia's hand, bringing the vampire comfort. "Like I was saying, Papa was distraught by what happened, and Mama told him that quote. It seemed to bring him something… comfort, a sense of meaning to what happened. I don't know." The young woman paused as she thought about her next words. "You and Lucian and Thad are doing the same on a huge scale. All of you are able to do unbelievable things to protect innocent people. Some of those things are violent, but I don't think that can be helped."

Warmth spread through Livia's heart. Her lips turned up. "Your parents raised you well. I remember your mama promising me she would when I handed you to her for the first time."

A blush crept up Cassie Lynn's cheeks. "You knew them? They never told me... though, I never asked. I thought it would hurt them that I wanted to know."

"They were outside the room while I was giving birth. They've sent me photos for years, and I have every one. They kept me going through many a dark time, human and vampire." Cassie Lynn's eyes glittered with tears. Livia wrapped her arms around her, and then looked her in the face. "Speaking of your parents, they're worried sick about you."

The young woman wiped her hands across her cheeks, shame making her avoid eye contact. "I left them a voicemail..."

"I somehow think that wasn't enough." Livia laughed softly. "And you know it." Cassie Lynn let out a dejected sigh. "Stay tonight. Sleep. Aidan will get you on the road safely in the morning."

Chapter Twenty-Nine

Loose Ends

Sinead Moss let out a breath as she placed the lid on the last cardboard box with her items in it. She gave the office one more glance to confirm she'd packed everything.

"The end of an era," Mike Ashe said, rolling his empty coffee mug back and forth between his palms.

She gently punched him on his upper arm. "It was a damn fine era, too." Her throat tightened as she looked up at her former partner. He tried to hide his sadness, but it was obvious in his eyes and the way his shoulders slumped. They'd been part of a team for almost a decade, and they'd been fast friends and confidants to one another. Her decision to leave the FBI had hit him hard.

"You're sure this is the right thing?"

"Yes... I don't know, Mike." She leaned her backside against the desk and crossed her arms over her chest. "When I woke up in that hospital and found out what had happened, I realized how I let this duty I felt I had consume my life, my family. I blindly walked into an active terrorist event, no thought for anything, no protection. I know that's what we're trained for but—" A nervous laugh escaped. "I have to do this. I have to take this second chance I now have with my family, to watch Lydia grow up."

A corner of his mouth twisted knowingly. "Yeah." His wife hadn't waited as long as Sinead's husband had to file for divorce. His Adam's apple bobbed as he swallowed hard. "You did a hell of a lot of good here."

"You're acting like you'll never see me again." Sinead shook her head, smiling. "There'll be hell to pay if Lydia doesn't see Uncle Mike once in a while." She wrapped her arms around him. "Just don't let this job consume you." She turned away before the tears she felt building could fall, grabbed the box, and left without turning around.

ও◈

Cassie Lynn turned the key and opened the door to the house, closing it behind her.

"Cassandra Lynn Monroe. Where the *hell* have you been?"

Her mouth became a desert at the worry in her father's voice. She turned, meeting the concerned faces of her parents. "Oh, um… didn't you get my message?"

Her father nodded and held up his cellphone, playing the message. *"Hiya. I'm, um, heading down to West Virginia with some, um, friends from school. I'll, um, call when I can. Love you guys!"*

Cassie Lynn cringed at the sound of her own voice and how it faltered at the half truths she had included.

"You know how many times I heard something like that as the *last* message parents ever got from their children? Do you?" Her father shook, from fear or anger, Cassie Lynn couldn't tell.

"I… I didn't think… I thought I'd be home sooner…" She gazed down at the floor and drew circles with the toe of her shoe.

Her mother's relief overcame her anger, and she embraced her daughter. "Where did you go? Why didn't you call, text… anything, honey?"

She swallowed hard, her stomach churning. "I went to Belle Hollow," she breathed. *There's no winning here. I can't tell them the absolute truth. They'll think I'm crazy.*

Her mother stepped back, her hands fumbling for the arm of the chair behind her as she sat. "Oh." Her face fell.

Cassie Lynn's father eased himself down on the arm of the chair, putting his hand on his wife's back. Their eyes met for a silent moment.

Cassie Lynn's gaze flitted between them as they focused back on her.

"You've, uh, wanted to go there for a long time, huh?" her father asked.

"Yeah." She inhaled, held the breath, and released it. Her heart hammered. "It… you guys said it wouldn't be a good vacation spot and wouldn't take me… but it was more than that, wasn't it?"

Her mother's mouth became a thin, white line; tears spilled over her cheeks. She nodded sharply, burying her face in her hands.

"Mama, no, don't cry." Cassie Lynn dropped to her knees in front of the woman. "It's not… I was curious." Relief washed over her as the lie came confidently out of her mouth. "But I was afraid to ask, didn't want you guys to think… I don't know. That I loved you less because I was curious."

Her mother's hands slipped away from her face. She reached out and tucked a lock of Cassie Lynn's hair behind her ear. "Why now? You've never asked, never seemed to have any interest in finding out."

Cassie Lynn sat back on her heels and stared down. "After being on that plane, I wanted to know… more about who I am." *Not a complete lie, I went there to find out what had happened. And I learned so much more than I bargained for.* "Being on that plane, experiencing that… changed me." *Definitely not a lie…*

"It does." A corner of her father's mouth lifted in sympathy. "But you still could have come to us. We would have told you everything you wanted to know." The man laughed quietly, his wife's face softening as she joined in.

"We found it ironic that you've been enthralled with Livia's work since you started acting. Nature will out." The woman studied her daughter, tilting her head to the side. "Did you get to meet her? Talk?"

Cassie Lynn's face lit up. "Yes. She's amazing…" *In an amazing world filled with vampires that I can never tell you about.* "And gave me an amazing life when she chose you and Papa to raise me."

ই৽ঌ৾

"… *Global rates of terrorism have dropped by fifty percent in the last year, though there are still places in the Middle East that remain hotbeds of radical activity. However, researchers are hopeful that this will be a continuing worldwide downtrend…*"

René Descoteaux caught random words from the news broadcast his wife was listening to in the kitchen, but his attention was focused on the baby he gently bounced on his thigh. The boy giggled uncontrollably as his grandfather made faces and blew raspberries. René lifted him above his head, the child's hazel eyes lighting up in delight. "Who's a big boy?" He eased him back down on his lap, petting the boy's dark hair. "That's right, you are!"

Joy washed through René as he watched his grandson coo and gurgle. "Do you know who you're named for?" he whispered, pulling a photo out of his back pocket. The little boy's arms worked up and down in excitement, though he didn't know the young man in the photos his grandfather held up. "Your *maman* and papa named you after someone very special, Sèbastien."

René's eyes roamed over the photos, taking in the half smile his eldest son wore as he held up his wine glass to the photographer and the look of love gracing his face as he danced with the redheaded woman. *I don't know who you are, but you saved me.*

He started, glancing behind him as a hand rested on his shoulder. His daughter Alix studied the photos from behind him.

"Who is that?" she asked, pointing to the woman dancing with her brother.

René handed her the photos, shaking his head, and tickling his grandson's belly. *"Je ne sais pas,"* he answered turning his head back. "They were left at the mausoleum months back."

A smile spread across Alix's face. "I knew he was hiding a girlfriend from me! Sneaky devil!" She moved the photo behind the other and stared down at the one of Bastien alone. Her lips turned down as she blinked back tears. Her fingers slid over her brother's face. "I miss him, Dad."

René cradled his grandson in one arm and stood, wrapping the other around his daughter. "We all do, Alix." The words from the letter he had found by his son's tomb flowed through his mind. "But Bastien wasn't one for grief, and he'd want us to be happy, especially now." He kissed the boy in his arms, then passed him to his daughter.

Alix took her nephew as he reached out for her. "Fèlicien chose a beautiful name."

Her father nodded. "May he live in a world more peaceful than what we have."

Epilogue

Bridget rested her forehead against the cold marble of Bastien's tomb and closed her eyes, thankful to have a moment of respite from the war she'd been waging for nearly a year.

Bastien wrapped his arms around her, the warmth of his skin enveloping her. She kissed his chest, the taste of calvados and his salt lingering on her lips. Her eyes closed as she remembered the soft grunts that left him as their lovemaking ended. His taste, his scent, his sounds, his feel. Soon this would be forever.

"All I want is to crawl in there with what's left of you, to be close to you again, but I've set something in motion." Her fingers blindly traced the letters etched in the stone. "Now I can't rest, take a long sleep like I loved doing when the modern world overwhelmed me." His features displayed vividly in her mind: the hazel eyes, his oh-so-slightly too long nose, the way his smile played on his lips when he looked at her. A soft laugh left her. "You changed me in so many ways. It's beautiful and cruel at once, what's happened to me, to the world."

She let the wall in her mind slide down, allowing a tsunami of visions to wash over her. Her knees buckled, bringing her down on all fours. Blood dripped from her nose onto the stone floor beneath her palms, her brain burning with the onslaught of information. "It's never-ending…" Crimson tears mingled with the pooled blood below her. She closed herself off, sobbing.

"It never does end." Fingers gently ran over her hair and back.

Bridget turned toward the voice, meeting soft tourmaline eyes. "Kali?" she breathed.

Kali wrapped her arms around Bridget, easing her away from the blood. "It never ends and it never will." She rested her lips on Bridget's forehead, wisps of her mahogany hair tickling the Elder's cheeks. "But you're making a difference."

"It feels like I've done nothing. I'm exhausted." Bridget covered her face, overwhelmed by the Original's presence, the ancient strength so close to her. "And sorry. Humans have found out about us because of this. Is that why you're here? To have me fix it?" The memories of being an enforcer rushed to her mind: endless nights spent stalking other vampires and humans and the terror of those she was sent to dispatch.

Kali moved Bridget's hands from her eyes. "No. What you're doing is too important to take you from."

"Then… why are you here?" Bridget's gaze moved over Kali's face in confusion.

The corners of Kali's mouth turned up softly. "To strengthen you, *Mo Cheann Beag*. It's something I shouldn't have waited so long to do." The Original sat back, pulling Bridget onto her lap, and offered her wrist.

Bridget hesitated before cradling Kali's hand in hers. She brought it up to her lips, resting them there and inhaling the comforting, warm scent of the Original. Her fangs pierced the skin, letting a sweet flood of cardamon, ginger, cinnamon, and black pepper slip over her tongue. Dizzying strength spread through her limbs. She closed her eyes and sat back, her bone-deep exhaustion fading like a dream.

"Rest awhile, let my blood do its job. Then you can get back to your war." Kali kissed Bridget's temple, running her fingers over her hair.

Bridget relaxed back, dozing against the Original's breast.

"*Kissed by the flames, you are, my love, take my hand and follow. We'll conquer all we see, my love. And bring life to the fire. Cross this river with me, my copper-haired child…*"

The End

About the Author

S.L. Baron isn't a full-time writer but keeps wishing she could quit her day job. She's been scribbling down stories since she was a small child, and she's glad the evidence of those stories no longer exists. After reading Anne Rice's *Interview With The Vampire*, she found her Muse. She's been obsessed with vampires and other types of immortals ever since. When she's not writing about her own Children of the Night, she reads all she can get her hands on about these and other supernatural creatures.

S.L. grew up near the shore in the New Jersey Pinelands but lives in West Virginia. She graduated from West Virginia University with a Bachelor of Arts in psychology. Keeping her company is her partner in crime, Tim, and three insane cats.

You can follow her on Twitter and Facebook @AuthorSLBaron, on Instagram @authorslbaron, and at her website, authorslbaron.com. If you enjoyed this book, please leave a review on Amazon, Barnes and Noble, Goodreads, and anywhere else you can spread the love!